Hunter stepped forward. "One night. No history. No interruptions. Just me and you."

"A date?" Her question was a whisper.

His hand reached up, gently grasping one of her curls. Something about the way he caressed her hair made her ache for his touch. "What do you say, Jo?" His eyes met hers. Blazing, electric, the pull almost physical. He released the curl, placing his big hands on either side of her head.

She blew out a shaky breath, unable to hide the effect he was having on her. His mouth was so close, his breath caressing her skin. His gaze explored her face, slow and intense. She tilted her head to him, an unmistakable invitation. Her heart kicked into overdrive as he leaned forward. She closed her eyes, waiting, ready, willing, bursting.

His forehead rested against hers.

"I'm not going to kiss you until you say yes," he rasped.

Her eyes popped open. "Yes," she answered quickly, too quickly. Not that there was any point in denying what was happening. They both felt it, they both wanted it.

He smiled and stepped away from her. "I'll pick you up at seven o'clock."

A Cowboy's Christmas Reunion

SASHA SUMMERS

Sasha Summers is part gypsy. Her passions have always been storytelling, romance and travel. Whether it's an easy-on-the-eyes cowboy or a hero of mythic proportions, Sasha falls a little in love with each and every one of her heroes. She frequently gets lost with her characters in the world she creates, forgetting those everyday tasks like laundry and dishes. Luckily, her four brilliant children and her hero-inspiring hubby are super understanding and helpful.

To the women who cheer me on
and keep me writing: Allison Collins,
Joni Hahn, Jolene Navarro,
Storm Navarro and Marilyn Tucker.

Pamela Hopkins, thank you for being
the best agent a gal could wish for.
Your belief in me means the world.

To my generous and funny editor,
Johanna Raisanen. I'm so very proud
to be a Mills & Boon author.
Thank you for making this experience
a dream come true!

And to my amazing family—
you make every day special.

Chapter One

She'd know that butt anywhere. Hunter Boone.
Damn it.

In eleven years, his derriere hadn't changed much. Lean hips and a tight butt hugged by work-faded Wrangler blue jeans. And, apparently, the view still managed to take her breath away. Which was unfortunate because she'd come home believing he couldn't affect her anymore—not even a little bit. She had been 110 percent confident that Hunter was out of her system. She was so wrong.

Her hands tightened on the tray she held and her lungs emptied as a memory of the way that rear felt under her hands…

She sighed, completely trapped.

This was not the reaction she'd expected after so long. Or the way she wanted to see him again. It...it pissed her off.

This isn't fair.

"Need some help with that, Josie?" Her father's voice made her wince.

She was hiding, clutching a tray of her dad's famous German breakfast kolaches and Danish, and crouching behind the display counter. Why was she—a rational, professional woman—ducking behind a bakery counter? Because *he'd* walked in and thrown her confidence in her face—a face whose forehead was currently streaked with flour and sugar and who knew what else.

There was no doubt her father's amused question had made all eyes in Pop's Bakery turn toward her. All eyes, even the very dazzling blue-green ones she was trying so desperately to avoid. There wasn't much to do about it now.

She shot her father a look as she said, "Nope, thanks, Dad. I've got it."

Her father winked, looking downright giddy. He'd known exactly what he was doing, and, knowing him, he could hardly wait to see what happened next.

Taking a deep breath, she stood slowly and slid the tray of breakfast goods into the display cabinet with intentional care. She refused to look at anything except the pastries. Or the stuffed deer head over the front door. That always made her smile—not that she was a fan of taxidermy. But her father insisted on decorating it for the seasons. It wore a red Santa hat. Ornaments dangled off its antlers, which were finished off with some tinsel and blinking twinkly Christmas lights. *Only in Stonewall Crossing, Texas.*

"I couldn't tell," her father continued. "You were all bent over, trying to balance that tray."

Josie's cheeks felt warm, but she wasn't about to admit she'd been hiding. "All good."

"Josie? Josie Stephens?" a high-pitched voice

asked. "Oh, my God, look at you. Why, you haven't changed since high school."

Josie glanced over the display case at the woman speaking. Josie couldn't place her, so she smiled and said, "Thanks. You, too."

That's when her gaze wandered to Hunter. He was waiting. And, from the look on his face, he *knew* Josie had no idea who the woman was. Which irritated her. Him, standing there, looking like *that*, irritated her.

This morning gets better and better.

First one of the ovens died, then she'd argued with her dad over which pills he was supposed to take, her dad's dog, Sprinkles, had buried one of her shoes somewhere in the backyard and now this. Hunter Boone, gorgeous and tall and manly and still too-perfect, looking at her. *The front view is just as good*—bad—*as the back.*

He smiled—bright blue-green eyes sparkling, damn dimple peaking in full force. She swallowed the huge lump in her throat. Not that she could have said anything if she'd wanted to.

"So it's true?" the woman continued. "Your dad said you were coming to help him, but I couldn't imagine you back *here*. We *all* know how much you hated Stonewall Crossing." Her speech pattern, the snide condescension, the narrowed eyes. Josie remembered her then. Winnie. Winnie Michaels. "What did you call it, redneck hell—right?"

Josie watched Hunter frown at Winnie's question, the slight shake of his head. It was all so familiar, unsettling, confusing. She blinked, turning her attention to the deer head and its flashing holiday cheer.

"Guess hell froze over." Winnie kept going, teasing—but with a definite edge.

"Kind of hard to say no when your dad needs you," Josie answered, forcing herself not to snap. Instead, she smiled. "I'm here."

"She wasn't about to let her old man try to run this place on his own." Her father jumped to her defense. "No matter how busy her life might be."

Busy didn't come close to describing her mess

of a life, but her dad didn't need more stress right now.

Her father dropped his arm around her shoulders and squeezed. "She's always been a daddy's girl."

She arched an eyebrow and shot him a look. "Are you complaining?"

Her father laughed. "Nope."

"I didn't think so." She kissed his cheek. "Now go *sit* down."

He shouldn't be up, but she knew better than to think he'd stay in his chair or use a walker. That was why she'd flown home from Washington, to take care of him. And because she needed someplace quiet to think things over.

"You know that's not going to happen, Jo." Same voice, same smile, same butt, same irritating nickname that only he used.

"*That's* why I'm here." Josie was thrilled she sounded completely cool, calm and collected. Her heart, on the other hand, was beating like crazy.

"It's kinda weird to see the two of you standing here." Winnie glanced back and forth between Josie and Hunter. "I mean, without having your tongues down each other's throats and all."

"Well—" Josie stared at the woman, then Hunter. He wasn't smiling anymore. His jaw was rigid, the muscles knotted. *Interesting.* "It's kind of hard with the display case in the way," she teased.

Hunter was quick. "I could jump over."

Josie shrugged, but her heart was on the verge of exploding. It was all too easy imagining him sliding across the glass-top counter, pulling her into his strong arms and— *Not going there.* "Nah. You don't want to break Dad's case."

"I don't mind," her father murmured, for her ears only, as he retreated to his chair.

Hunter shook his head. "I think we'll have to wait for now." He cocked his head, eyes still pinned on Josie. "I've gotta get these kolaches to the boys."

Josie saw him take the huge box by the register. A swift kick of disappointment prompted her to blurt out, "Too bad, Hunter. If I remember it correctly, you knew how to kiss a girl."

He smiled again, shaking his head. "If you remember? Ouch. Guess I've had some competition the last few years." His eyes swept her face, lingering on her lips just long enough to make her cheeks feel hot.

She knew better but didn't say a word.

Hunter inclined his head ever so slightly. "Thanks, Carl. I'll see you later on. Have fun while you're back in hell, Jo. I'll see you around."

That would be a bad idea.

Josie watched him leave. His back—and butt—disappeared as he climbed into the driver's side of a huge dark blue one-ton extended cab truck. She saw him wink at her then and shook her head, a familiar ache pressing in on her. *Time doesn't heal all wounds.* How many hours had she spent wishing she hadn't pushed him away? That she hadn't set him up for failure, because she had… No point in rehashing it again.

She turned back to the display counter to arrange the pastries she'd made at four-thirty this morning. Dad's fall had shaken them both. He was the last stable thing she had left. He needed her—that was the only reason she'd come home. The last thing she wanted was to be back exactly where she'd been eleven years ago, working in her father's bakery in a town she couldn't wait to escape. Yes, she'd hoped coming back would dispel some of her fantasies about Hunter Boone. And, if she was really lucky, she could finally get her heart back. After seeing Hunter again, one thing was certain. As soon as her dad didn't need her, she was gone.

HUNTER PUT THE TRUCK in Reverse and blew out a slow breath as he craned his head to check his blind spot.

"Was that her?" Eli asked, his voice and eyes cold.

Hunter glanced at his son but wasn't up for an argument. "That's Jo."

"She's not that pretty," Eli grumbled.

"No? I think she is." His voice was neutral. Pretty didn't come close to describing Jo Stephens. Silver-gray eyes, wild curly hair, with curves to drive a man to drink. She was beautiful. There wasn't a man alive who wouldn't admit that. Except his son. "And she's funny. Really funny."

"Huh." Eli wasn't impressed.

Hunter knew Eli's blue-green eyes—eyes his boy got from him—were watching him. He could feel Eli's anger—over Jo. But there wasn't much to say.

Amy, Eli's mom, had done too good a job of trashing Jo. And as much as he'd like Eli to believe that Jo had nothing to do with the bitter end of his marriage to Amy, he knew better. Jo Stephens had held his heart since he was sixteen. And he didn't mind too much. Seeing her this morning was like downing a pot of coffee—

"Did you get enough for everyone?" Eli interrupted.

Hunter smiled at his son. "I don't know. But I got a lot."

Eli grinned. "We're growing boys, Dad."

"I know, kid." Hunter looked at Eli, taking in the slight sharpening of his features. His son was growing up. There were still traces of roundness on his ten-year-old body. In no time, his son would be all arms and legs, big feet and teen-age awkwardness.

He was a good-looking boy. And in the years ahead, Eli Boone was going to be a good-looking man. More important, he was smart and kind and had solid common sense. Hunter was proud of that.

He'd done the best he could by his son. The two of them took care of each other with little complaining. Balancing his son, the ranch and teaching at the university veterinary hospital was hard work, but it was worth it. No matter what, he made sure Eli *suffered* through every school trip to the opera, the museums or any-where else that broadened his son's horizons.

He knew there was a big world out there, and he wanted Eli to know it, too. He wouldn't have his mistakes cause his son to miss out on anything.

"Uncle Fisher gonna make it to this one?" Eli asked.

"He said he'd be there." Hunter nodded. And his brothers always kept their word.

Eli nodded, too, then said, "Dara thinks she's gonna get a one."

"She can dream, can't she?" he teased gently.

Dara Greer had joined the local Future Farmers of America club this year. Her family had moved from the city and her folks wanted her to "fit in." Problem was she was nervous around animals and uncomfortable in the show ring.

"I know." Eli grew thoughtful. "But she's sweet. And she's trying really hard. You know?"

Hunter looked at his son with a new sense of understanding. "Oh?"

Eli nodded, red streaking up his neck and coloring his face. "Y-yeah." He pushed his dad on the shoulder, laughing.

Hunter turned back to driving. He knew. Boy, did he know.

Jo had been a lot like Dara when she'd moved to town. She was this guarded, thoughtful type whose gaze seemed to search his soul. Every attempt he made to get her attention had earned him an eye roll or a shake of her curly-haired head. She'd hated his "boot-wearing, deer-shooting ass." He'd teased her for her Hunting is Murder T-shirts. And her lightning-fast comebacks had driven him crazy. They'd fought, long and loud, refusing to admit the other might have a point or a right to their own perspective.

But when he'd grabbed her in the high school agriculture barn, her kiss had set his blood on fire. He was done for even if she was still hesitant. He didn't know then that Jo didn't believe in love, romance or commitment. Mostly because she'd never seen it. Her mom had changed husbands more often than most women had their hair done. Moving in with her dad, to Stonewall

Crossing, was a way to get away from the drama and uncertainty she'd grown to hate.

It had taken him a long time to get her to trust him, for her to believe he was hers. Sure, they'd still argued, all the time, but they'd been just as quick to make up.

Some things were just too big to forgive.

When she'd left, when she'd had to leave, half of his heart had gone with her. The other half had gone to Eli.

Josie ran to the phone, slipping once on the water her hair was sprinkling all over the tile floor. Only her dad would still have one house phone, with a cord no less, placed in the middle of the hallway. Sprinkles sat, staring at the phone, barking and howling.

"Hush, Sprinkles." She answered the phone. "Hello?"

"Jo?" Of course he would call her while she was in the shower.

Sprinkles kept yapping. "Shh." She took a deep breath. "Um, hi, Hunter."

"You okay? You sound kinda out of breath?"

"I'm in— I was in the shower." She laughed airily. "I'm making a puddle on Dad's floor as we speak." Why was she sharing that information with him?

He chuckled. "Want me to call you back?"

Sprinkles jumped up.

"I'm out now." The dog howled. "Sprinkles!" Sprinkles sat, staring at her. She ignored Hunter's laugh. "What's up?" Not that she wanted to know why he'd called...

"I was wondering how long you were going to be here." He sounded hesitant.

"At least through Christmas... Then see how Dad is. Why?"

"Well, the FFA chapter here always builds a Christmas float and some of the parents thought it might be nice to build one around your books."

"Oh." She didn't know what to say.

"I'm in my truck right now—" He paused.

"And I'm about to go by your place. Can I come in and show you what they came up with?"

"Oh, um…" *I'm just wrapped in a towel and dripping wet.* "Well…"

"Okay. See you in a sec." And he hung up.

"Damn it." She glared at the handset. "Damn it, damn it."

Sprinkles barked.

"Joselyn Marie Stephens," her father chastised her from the living room.

"Really, Dad?" She peered around the corner to find her father sitting in his recliner. "You're right there and you couldn't get the phone? And I'm almost thirty. I can say damn it. I could even say—"

There was a knock on the door. Sprinkles started barking like mad.

"Someone stopping by?" he asked.

"Shit," she squealed, then almost tripped over Sprinkles and ran back into the bathroom.

"Come in," she heard her dad call out. *Or go home.* She pulled her thick robe on and picked through her brown curls quickly. She rolled her eyes at her reflection. *Chill. Relax.* She straightened her shoulders and opened the door.

There was no help for it. She'd have to walk past the living room to get to her bedroom. Which meant Hunter would be treated to a view of her wrapped in her fluffy black-and-blue bathrobe. She could almost hear her mother scolding her. *A single woman must always look her best when keeping company with a handsome man.* Josie sighed, grabbed an extra towel and started drying up her watery path from the bathroom to the hall.

"Oh, hey." Hunter laughed. "You really were in the shower."

She turned, one eyebrow arched, all sarcasm. "What makes you say that?" A boy peered around Hunter then. And Josie felt her irritation slip.

This was him…Hunter's son. She felt pain. Pain she thought she'd worked through years ago. She stared at the boy.

The boy stared back. He had Hunter's intense gaze and startling eyes.

She held up a finger. "Let me get dressed."

"We're not going to stay long." Hunter's voice was soft.

She pulled her gaze from the boy, her toes curling into the area rug beneath her feet. "Well, you're going to have to give me a second because I refuse to have a conversation with someone while I'm wearing a robe. Okay?" And she needed a minute to get a grip. She half ran to her room, almost tripped over Sprinkles again and closed the door without a sound. "Shit," she murmured with feeling.

Dad needs me. That's why I'm here. I don't have to do this float or spend time with Hunter... or his beautiful son. But I do have to take care of Dad.

She pulled on her underwear and dug through the suitcase, then the piles of clothes all over her room. She sighed, pulling on a pair of jeans and a thermal shirt. A quick search unearthed her fuzzy pink bunny slippers, which she slipped on while she headed back to the waiting crew.

"It's the best I could do in two minutes," she muttered when she saw her father's disapproving glance. "I'll put on my hoopskirt and pearls next time, okay?"

The boy smiled briefly, while Hunter laughed.

"Nice to meet you." She stuck her hand out to the boy. She couldn't ignore him—she didn't want to. He looked like a Boone, which was a good thing. If he'd looked like Amy... She swallowed. "I'm—"

"Joselyn," her dad offered.

"Or Jo," Hunter added.

"Or Josie, even." She rolled her eyes.

"Eli," he said, shaking her hand quickly. He nodded and then sat by her father on the couch.

The door opened and Josie felt a moment's panic as she spun around. If it was Amy—

"Well, if it isn't Miss Joselyn Stephens." Two hands picked her up, holding her eye to eye with a large wall of a man.

"Fisher?" She couldn't believe this…this person was Hunter's little brother. "What happened to you?"

He smiled. "I drank milk." He pulled her into a bear hug.

"By the truckload?" She hugged him back. "You look great."

"I do." He nodded.

She giggled, stepping away from him as he put her on the ground. "At least your sense of humor hasn't changed."

"Not that I mind you all stopping by, but can we start over so I know what's going on?" her dad interrupted. He was a stickler for his routine. The bakery opened at six, so he was in bed by nine each and every evening. She glanced at the clock. It was ten after nine.

Hunter spoke first. "Christmas float time. FFA met tonight and came up with a few ideas. One of them was to build something around Josie's story characters."

Josie didn't know where to look. If she looked

at Hunter, she felt…all sorts of conflicting and overwhelming *things*. If she looked at Eli, she felt empty. And if she looked at her dad, she felt rumpled and unattractive. Fisher was her only option. He winked at her when she glanced his way. It helped.

"You don't have to tell *me* it's Christmastime. Christmas parade kicks off the Gingerbread Festival." Her father winked at her. "Which means Josie and I will be up to our elbows in the stuff for the next week."

"Can't wait." Josie smiled. "Bonding while baking is a family tradition." She made the terrible mistake of looking Hunter's way. Hunter, who was watching her. His crooked grin and cocked eyebrow stirred up a series of memories. A flash of him smiling at her while they floated down the river. Another of them lying on a blanket under the stars. Him teaching her to drive stick shift. Making love for the first time. *Not thoughts I need to have right now.* Her heart lodged itself in her throat.

"Family traditions are good." Fisher grinned. "Even better if it puts food on the table, right? A man's got to eat."

"Which characters?" her father asked, turning to Eli.

Eli shrugged. "Thirty-four, probably. Since some of us have calves."

"Thirty-four?" She tore her gaze from Hunter.

"It was Dad's calf, right?" Eli asked.

Josie nodded, rattled. "Yes, his state champion calf." Her gaze settled on Eli. He looked a lot like Hunter when they'd first met. Her heart hurt. "What can I do to help?"

"Well, we're gonna build the float. But they—we—were wondering…" Eli was clearly uncomfortable. "Would you ride on it?"

She shook her head. "Um, I hate the spotlight, Eli."

"It's just a parade." Eli's eyes were scornful. "In Stonewall Crossing."

"Come on, Josie," her father said. "You wrote books about this place, the town and people."

Fisher elbowed her. "You are a celebrity here, kind of."

"And it's for the kids," her dad added.

She held her hands up. "Really, Dad? You're going to play the for-the-kids card?"

Hunter laughed, sending a wave of awareness along her neck. "Nothing to add, H-Hunter?" She stumbled over his name. It was stupid. Not like she could call him Mr. Boone. *It's a name, for crying out loud.* Saying it shouldn't affect her, or send the slightest shiver down her spine.

His gaze traveled over her face before peering into her eyes. "You might make some good memories before you go back. Something for a new book."

She couldn't look away. And she really needed to look away. He might not be grappling with memories, with need and want, but she sure as hell was.

"Come on, Josie. Live a little," Fisher added.

She should say no, but Hunter had found her weakness. A new book… Wouldn't that be something? Not that anyone knew she was in the midst of the longest creative drought of her career. That's why she was considering the teaching position in New Mexico. She wanted to feel inspired again.

Maybe working on the float could help. At this point, it couldn't hurt. Her career, anyway.

"So?" Eli's question ended her tortured introspection.

"Yes." She smiled at Eli as she spoke. "Thanks, Eli. I mean, it's nice to feel special for my stories." *Don't ask. Don't ask.* But she did. "Did you ever read them?" Thinking about Amy reading her stories to Eli made her stomach twist.

Eli looked at his dad. "Dad used to read me *34* and *Floppy Feet* all the time."

Fisher snorted. "Hey, hey, now. I've read the cow one—"

"It's called *34*," Hunter answered.

"Right, *34*." Fisher nodded at his brother. "A time or two, Eli."

Eli grinned at his uncle.

Josie risked another glance at Hunter, but he was staring into the fire with a small smile on his face.

"That reminds me, Josie, Annabeth called from the elementary school earlier. She wants you to do a story time there." Her father spoke up.

"I'd love that." She smiled. Other than her father, Annabeth was the only one in Stonewall Crossing she'd kept in touch with after she'd left.

Hunter looked at her, his voice soft as he said, "The kids would, too, Jo."

Jo. For an instant she wanted him to grab her and kiss her, just as he used to. When he'd kissed her, nothing else mattered. She nodded, staring into his eyes wordlessly.

"We should go, Dad. I've got a math test Monday morning." Eli stood up. "Thanks for helping us out…Miss Stephens."

She turned away from Hunter and beamed at the boy. "You really can call me Josie, Eli, please. I don't like feeling old."

"Yes, ma'am." He barely glanced at her, his answering smile forced. "Thanks for the breakfast this morning, Mr. Stephens."

"How'd you do?" her father asked.

"Eli got a one at the stock show." Hunter smiled at his son, placing a hand on the boy's shoulder. "He's been working real hard with Bob, his steer. And the judges could tell."

It was clear Hunter was a devoted father, just as she'd always known he'd be. Something hard settled in the pit of her stomach, a hollow, empty ache.

"I wasn't the only one." Eli's cheeks were red. "Now there's nothing big until after Christmas."

"Time to get ready for the next one." Her father winked at the boy. "You should be proud, Eli."

"Thank you, sir." Eli nodded and headed for the door.

"Don't get up," Josie said to her dad.

"Now, Josie—" her father started to argue.

"Dad." She held her hand up.

"We know the way out. Don't get Jo all worked

up." Hunter shook her father's hand. "Have a good evening, Carl. Thanks for having us over."

Her dad winked. "You're welcome anytime, Hunter. You know that. You, too, Fisher."

She knew her father cared for Hunter—he always had. After all, Hunter had been almost family. Her gut twisted. She led Hunter to the door, needing him to go—now.

"I know you're a big-time author now, but I expect to see you some before you go." Fisher hugged her again before following Eli out and into the truck.

Hunter lingered in the doorway. His gaze wandered over her face. "You and Carl want to come out to the ranch tomorrow? Have dinner with us? I've made a lot of changes."

Josie stared at him, surprised. Did she want to go? No, she really didn't. It would be awkward and painful. *Us.* She didn't think she could handle seeing his family unit together, in a place she'd truly loved. Where Amy now lived. "I don't—"

But her father interrupted her, loudly. "Sounds good."

No, it doesn't. It sounds like a nightmare. She mumbled, "Are you sure that's okay?"

Hunter smiled that crooked smile. "It's my home. Of course it's okay. See you about six?"

She stood there, searching for some sort of excuse, while he climbed into his truck and drove away.

Chapter Two

Hunter didn't say much on the drive back to the ranch. Fisher, who was never at a loss for words, kept Eli talking all things steers and Future Farmers of America. And Hunter was thankful for it. Spending time with Jo was harder than he'd expected. Leaving her was worse. If he could get her alone, if he could talk to her... What would he say? He was eleven years too late to apologize.

Fisher said good-night and headed to his place, leaving Eli to his homework and Hunter to his paperwork.

"I guess she is kinda pretty." Eli sounded thoughtful.

"Who?" Hunter looked at his son over his laptop.

"Josie." Eli gazed at the homework spread out on the table all around him. He tapped his pencil on the table, then added, "I guess I sorta get it. But Mom's prettier."

Hunter looked at his son. "Your mom is beautiful, Eli." Amy had always been pretty—to look at. But her beauty was skin-deep. Underneath was something else entirely.

No point being negative. Chances are she'd be coming through town for the holidays. Sometimes it went well, sometimes it didn't. But he wanted his son to have a relationship with his mom, no matter how he felt about his ex-wife.

"So are you going to date her?"

Hunter looked at his son again. "What?"

"Are you going to date Josie?" Eli's bright eyes challenged his father unflinchingly.

"No." No matter how much he wanted to. "She'll be heading back after the holidays, anyway." He kept his voice neutral.

"If she wasn't leaving, would you?" Eli's gaze continued to burn into his.

Hunter studied his son for a long time. "Yes," he answered truthfully. "But I don't know if she'd want to date me, kid. It's not that easy, you know?"

"Why?" His son's eyes narrowed a little.

He hedged. "It's just not. Women are…complicated."

Eli sighed and looked back at his homework. "I know."

Hunter stared at the top of his son's head. "What does that mean?"

"Woman *are* complicated." Eli was bright red when he looked at his father. "I asked Dara if she'd have lunch with us…at the county show."

Hunter bit back his smile. "Did she say no?"

Eli shook his head, then shrugged. "She didn't say anything."

"You should ask her again. You might have surprised her. What did you say?"

"I don't know." He paused, thinking. "Something like, 'Have lunch with me at the next show.'"

Hunter nodded, fighting the urge to laugh.

"She just stood there, staring at me." Eli looked at his paper.

"Did you ask her or tell her?"

Eli tapped his pencil again. "I think I asked her."

"Ask her again."

Eli frowned at his paper, the pencil tapping faster. "It's no big deal. I gotta get this done."

"Need help?"

Eli shook his head.

Hunter sat, trying to stare at his computer. His son had his first crush and he didn't know what to tell him. He thought Dara was a nice enough girl, but they were both so young. And shy. Eli had probably scared the shit out of her, at the very least surprised her. But Hunter knew better than to push. If Eli was done talking about it, then they were done talking about it. Eli had homework and so did he.

He had a good group of fourth-year vet students, partly because he was so hard on them. The semester might be winding down, but clinical rotations weren't. Not like the patients disappeared because it was winter break. If his students didn't like it, they could take a look at the long waiting list of eager candidates waiting for any open spot to remind them of how lucky they were to be there, working through the holidays.

He leaned back in his chair, propped his feet up and logged on to the University of East Texas website, then the College of Veterinary Medicine intranet to access his files. He had two classes of finals to grade and his caseload of patient files to review. His fourth-year students were doing most of the patient charting, but he had to check each and every note.

Most were spays and neuters. A couple of dogs with parvovirus. He glanced over their charts. Poor dogs had to be isolated and hooked up to an IV to keep hydrated. It was expensive to cure and messy to treat. All it took was one easy vaccination to prevent the whole thing.

He clicked ahead, skimming the fourth years' notes. No errors so far. He closed those files, then opened Mars's file. They were all getting attached to the sweet yellow Labrador. She'd been with them for two weeks now. Her owners had carried her in, bleeding and limp, after she'd been hit by a car. He hoped her paralysis was temporary, but the dog wasn't improving the way he'd expected. They'd have to perform a cesarean soon. He didn't have much hope for the three puppies she carried, but he prayed Mars survived. He added a note to schedule the surgery for next week and closed the file.

"Dad," Eli said. "Did Uncle Fisher get the four-wheelers back?"

"Yes." He glanced at his son. "But you're not driving them."

"Uncle Fisher would let me." Eli frowned. "And Uncle Archer and Uncle Ryder would let me, too."

"They might. But they're not your father." He nodded. "You'd best not bother them about it too much, or you'll end up working this weekend."

Eli smiled. "They wouldn't make me do that. I'm their favorite nephew."

"You're their only nephew." He chuckled.

"Harsh, Dad." He laughed, too, then turned back to his homework.

"You'll always be their favorite." He worried about teasing his son sometimes.

"I know." Eli arched an eyebrow, grinning.

Hunter shook his head, but he smiled. God, he loved his boy.

He was lucky—he knew it. He had a job he loved. The research he and his brothers had been doing on the ranch had led to a partnership with the state agricultural agency. Their hard work and dedication had made Boone Ranch one of the biggest conservation and rehabilitation sites in this part of the country. They'd had a plan, a good plan. And once Hunter had a plan, he stayed with it until the end.

Losing Jo hadn't been part of the plan. And nothing had ever hurt like that.

Jo.

He fisted his hands, wishing he could stop wanting her, needing her. She was here, so close, yet still out of his reach. Seeing her now reminded him of everything he'd had and lost. Thinking about her wouldn't bring her back, wouldn't change what he'd done—

"Do you still love her, Dad?" Eli was looking at him.

He hadn't realized that he wasn't looking at his computer anymore. His gaze had wandered, and he'd been blindly staring out the window.

"I'm supposed to go to Tommy's house tomorrow night. Remember?" Eli asked. "Don't want to leave you alone if it'll be…weird," Eli finished.

Fisher had already told them he wouldn't be coming, but he hadn't offered up an explanation.

Hunter glanced at his son. "Guess it's a good thing her dad's coming for dinner, too."

"Why?" Eli asked.

"Because when Jo and I are alone, we tend to fight."

JOSIE WAS TIRED. And stressed. And tired of being stressed. And now she was getting a headache. Probably because she was heading to dinner with the love of her life and the only person she'd ever hated. Not hated…just actively disliked. That was why she'd made her father and Annabeth promise not to bring up anything to do with Amy. Or Hunter. She didn't like who she was, how she felt, where Amy was concerned.

"Holy crap," Josie breathed as she pulled through the huge stone entranceway, the intricate wrought-iron gate open wide. This was nothing like the Boone ranch she remembered. This was something else. She drove slowly, following the twisting limestone drive until she reached three outbuildings.

One was obviously a ranger station. It was elevated, with a two-story ladder the only way up. A small building sat next to it, a long ranch house of sorts with two large trucks parked beside it. Then there was the main building, several stories tall, all wood and native stone and rather impressive.

Almost as impressive as the man sitting on the porch. She sighed. Hunter sat, a laptop on his knees. He looked gorgeous—and a little bit dangerous to what remained of her heart.

She put the car in Park, trying not to stare as he smiled at her. He closed the laptop and walked down the steps to greet her.

The throbbing in her head was matched by the pounding of her heart. Whether it was from nerves or exhaustion, she didn't know. But watching him walk to her car did little to calm her nerves. It was going to be a long night.

She rolled down the passenger window as he leaned forward to say, "Hi."

"Hi." She forced a smile. "Dad bailed at the last minute." Which had led to a thirty-minute argument. At least Eli would be there as a buffer.

A strange look crossed Hunter's face and then he smiled. "His hip giving him trouble?"

"Yes." That's what her father had told her, though she suspected he was trying to play matchmaker. Why her father was trying to fix her up with a married man was a mystery. After the hell her mother's indiscretions had put him through, she'd expected him to place a little more value on the whole faithful vow thing. He'd always been on the eccentric side, but this was ridiculous. Hunter was off-limits, no if, ands or buts about it.

"Can you give me a ride?" he asked. "Or we can take some horses."

"How much farther is the main house?" She let her eyes travel over the buildings again. "And why don't I recognize any of this?"

His eyes traveled over her face. "Did you think you'd recognize it?"

"Of course." She rolled her eyes. "I mean, I figured you'd made some changes, and you obviously have, but…"

"I didn't own this when we… In high school this wasn't part of the family ranch. We bought this about six years ago." He paused.

"That makes sense. So, if I remember correctly, this must be the guest lodge?" She took it all in, impressed. "Am I right?" She waited for him to nod. "Well, wow, congratulations. Looks like your big plans are coming together."

"Most of them." He nodded, his eyes boring into hers. "So horses or driving?"

She looked down at her skirt. "Driving. Didn't know horses were part of the evening."

He opened the passenger door and climbed in. "Just stay on the drive to the left. It's a ways down yet."

She drove on, and her small red four-door rental seemed to shrink as the silence stretched on.

It was too quiet. The pounding in her head seemed to echo. "Too bad you didn't have paved roads when you taught me to drive. Maybe I wouldn't have totaled that truck."

"You didn't. That thing was like a tank." He looked at her. "It wasn't for a lack of trying, though."

"I guess I should blame my teacher." She flashed him a grin.

He chuckled. "Sure. If that makes you feel better about wrecking my granddad's truck, you just go on telling yourself that."

"God, I felt terrible." She shook her head. "I still do."

"Don't. Still drive it back and forth around here when I need to run errands or deliver something. Imagine I'll teach Eli to drive in it." Hunter rested his head against the headrest.

As they crested the next hill, Josie saw the ranch house. It had always been a special place, where her most treasured memories took place. She was hit with a case of nerves so intense she almost turned the car around. Instead, she did what she always did when she was nervous. She talked.

"You've made a lot of improvements to the

house. I knew you'd never tear it down, since your grandmother was born here." She paused, but he didn't say anything. "I guess it's nice to have some privacy for you and your family. I mean, you haven't said anything about the way the ranch works now, but I remember the way you said you wanted it to work. Population studies. Rehabilitation center. Animal preserve. Did you ever get the white-tail deer breeding program started?" Her head felt as if it had a band tightening around it. "Guess you're keeping cattle, too, since Eli is raising a calf?" She stopped as the car pulled up in front of the house. Crippling anxiety gripped her, the throbbing pulse around her skull excruciating.

Any second Amy was going to walk out that front door. Any second Hunter was going to put his arm around Amy, his wife, and they were all going inside to have a meal together. Why had she come? She felt very nauseous.

"You okay?" he asked.

She looked at him, watching the traces of

amusement turn into concern. "I'm not sure. I'm feeling a little…off."

His forehead creased as he stared at her face. "You're really pale." His hand touched her cheeks and forehead. His touch felt so good. "But you feel cool. Let's get you something to drink."

He climbed out of the car and walked around to her side. He opened the door, but she was paralyzed with fear.

"Maybe I should go home. I feel weird about leaving Dad home alone." Which was partly true.

"Okay," he said slowly. "You can leave. Once there's some color in your cheeks and you don't look like you're gonna pass out. Don't think this car would take a beating the way Granddad's truck did."

She glared up at him. She pinched her cheeks, then smiled thinly. "There. Color in my cheeks."

He laughed. "Don't make me pick you up, Jo."

She slipped from the car, grasping the roof for support.

They stood there, regarding each other in the warm rays of the setting sun. No one came out to greet them. Other than the faint coo of a dove, the moo of a distant cow and the slightly rhythmic whump of the windmill's blades, it was quiet.

"Drink?" he asked. He held out his hand awkwardly.

She stared at it and pushed off her car, not taking it. "I think I can manage to walk to the door, Hunter. I'll have my drink and hit the road and you can have a peaceful evening with the family."

"Eli's out." He sounded amused. "Fish, Archer and Ryder all have places of their own. But Renata still lives with Dad so she can take care of him. She always was a daddy's girl."

Josie felt bile in her throat. He wanted her to sit through dinner with him and Amy? She felt angry suddenly.

"Don't you think it might be a little awkward?" She turned toward him. "Okay, a *lot* awkward."

"Why?" He looked genuinely surprised. "Why would being alone with me be awkward?"

Josie was distracted by the shift of emotions on his face. The tone of his voice was soft but coaxing. He seemed to take a step toward her, rattling her from her silence.

"Alone?" A full-fledged pounding began at the base of her skull. Shooting pain focused right behind her left eye.

He nodded. "Let's get you inside. You can lie down, have your drink, and once you're better, you can leave, if that's what you want to do."

"I should go now," she argued. "Pretty sure it's a migraine and once it gets started—"

"You'll be down for the count." He nodded, slipping his arm around her for support. "You're not driving, Jo. It wouldn't be right or gentle-manly."

"You could be a gentleman and drive me home now." She didn't have the energy to argue, but she refused to lean into him.

"In a bit." He swung her up into his arms.

"Hunter—" His name escaped on a startled breath, right before she was bombarded with his scent. Everything about him was familiar. The earthy spice of him, the strength of his arms, the warmth he exuded, the feel of his breath against her forehead. It was sweet torture. "I can walk," she bit out, sitting rigidly in his arms. She would not relax. She would not melt in his arms and press herself to him. She would not kiss his neck or run her hands through his thick, dark blond hair. She would not think of doing those things, either.

He carried her into the house, ratcheting up her nerves. This was how she was going to see Amy? In his arms? Her whisper was urgent. "Please put me down."

And he did. On the couch. "Sit," he murmured before leaving the room.

"Bark bark," she muttered childishly. Her gaze bounced around the room, searching, waiting.

He laughed. "You still do that?"

"You still order people around?" she snapped.

He left and then walked back with a glass of water and a bottle of pain pills. He sat on the coffee table opposite the couch, offering them to her.

She stared at him, deciding whether to take the offered answer to her pain or suffer through out of sheer stubbornness. She took the bottle and the water.

"Still get migraines?" he asked.

She shrugged, pouring a couple of pain relievers into her hand before putting the lid back on the bottle. "Sometimes." She glanced at him. "Still have sneezing fits?"

"Sometimes." He smiled. "Still painting? I mean, other than your illustrations."

"Yes." It was ironic that, even though she'd been desperate to leave the state of Texas and everything about it, Texas landscapes were one of her favorite things to paint. "Still write poetry?"

"No." He stared down at her. "You wanna lie down? Eli's room is a mess, but you can rest in mine if you want."

Rest in his room? *Amy's room?*

She shook her head. "No, thank you. If I lie here for a minute, will you let me leave?"

He stood over her, still smiling. "I'm not kidnapping you, Jo. You can go whenever you want to go. As long as you can make it all the way back into town with no problems."

She sat up and felt instantly nauseous.

"Yeah." He sighed. "Stop being so stubborn and lie down."

"I'm stubborn?" she snapped as she lay back on the cushions of the couch.

"Relax for a few. Dinner's almost ready." He winked at her. "The protein'll do you some good."

She pulled her gaze from him, shaking her head. "Where is everyone again?" Being alone with him wasn't good for her. She didn't like feeling so vulnerable, so needy. As a matter a fact, she was feeling way too much right now. Even with her pounding head, she was preoccupied with thoughts of being wrapped in his arms.

"Eli's spending the night with a friend. My brothers have their own places. They're probably off doing what grown men do." Hunter shrugged.

"That sounds…dangerous," she muttered, waiting for the rest. But Hunter didn't say a thing about Amy. She narrowed her eyes. He was going to make her ask, wasn't he? She started to, but couldn't. It had taken her a long time not to wince just thinking Amy's name. She sure as hell wasn't going to say it, out loud, here.

She'd turn up sooner or later—she always did.

"No interruptions. You rest. I'll work. You can eat later and I'll drive you home."

She continued to glare at him, even as she lay back on the couch cushions. Her head was pounding, making her ears ring. She closed her eyes, trying to relax. But she couldn't.

She was alone with Hunter. Just the two of them. She opened her eyes, looking for him.

The place had changed, but it still felt the same. The inside had obviously been gutted and redone. The walls were painted a warm cream with knotty wood trim. The ceiling was dark, with heavy exposed beams. The cast-iron wagon-wheel chandelier was the same. So was the wood-burning stove in the far corner.

But the room felt bigger—was bigger. The dining room was now part of this room—separated by a long brown leather sofa. On the far wall, beneath a huge picture window, was Hunter's old-fashioned drafting table. Her mouth went dry at the memories that table stirred up.

They'd spent most of that morning bringing in the round hay bales in the tractor. Once they'd been left alone, she'd dragged him inside with obvious intentions. Her lips had fastened on his neck, tasting the salt of his sweat. When her lips suckled and nipped at his earlobe, he'd tugged her jeans off, tossing them hurriedly over his shoulder before grasping her hips and setting her onto the table. With his jeans around his ankles, he'd loved her hard and fast. How could she remember the feel of him, as though he was with her now?

They'd been young, too young… But they'd loved each other, really loved each other. And then life—Amy—had gotten in the way.

She swallowed. Her head was spinning. She needed to get the hell out of here. She needed to put as much space between them as possible. The only way to do that was to get rid of her headache.

She took a slow, steady breath and forced herself to relax against the pillows.

HUNTER SET THE TABLE as quietly as he could.

She'd been asleep for almost an hour. But he knew the longer she slept, the better she'd feel.

He moved to the couch and stared down at her.

The years hadn't touched her. She'd never been a fan of makeup, so her skin was still smooth and silky. She had some faint lines bracketing her mouth and eyes, where she crinkled when she laughed. And when she laughed, she looked so damn beautiful.

He ran a hand over his face, shaking his head. If he could go back in time, follow her, he would.

No, he wouldn't. Because then he wouldn't have Eli. And as much as he regretted losing Jo, he loved his son.

Jo stirred, her movements capturing his attention. Her mouth parted, then smiled slightly as she turned onto her side. There was a flutter of movement under her eyelids, and she sighed.

He spread the blanket from the back of the couch over her before heading into the kitchen. He turned down the stove and put the salad back in the refrigerator. Dinner would keep—she needed sleep.

Once he'd turned off all the lights, he went to his desk and opened his laptop. He glanced at her, then at the desk. He'd had to patch the lid after Amy had ripped it off at the hinges. She couldn't stand the *H.B. + J.S.* that he'd carved into the wood. Even though he'd been the one to replace the lid, he still looked for the carving whenever he opened the desk for supplies.

Did Jo have someone special? As much as he wanted her, he wanted her happiness more. He wondered if she'd made any other men as happy as she'd made him. She probably had. Eleven years was a long time to go without. And Jo was a passionate woman. He remembered that about her with great fondness.

Everything about her was like a living, breathing fire. From her sparkling eyes and lightning-fast humor to her equally fast temper and her instant and all-consuming desire. She'd been every young man's dream.

His gaze wandered back to her. She was still his dream.

A distant rumbling made him glance out the window. The sky was flashing. They needed the rain. There was a burn ban in effect and two fires had already claimed thousands of acres on surrounding properties. All it took was one asshole throwing his still burning cigarette butt out the window and, poof, a whole season's worth of work was up in smoke.

Maybe he should wake her. If it rained too hard too fast, the road would wash out and he wouldn't be able to get her back home. Not home, to Carl's, he reminded himself. She didn't live here anymore and Texas had never been her idea of home. He'd thought he might be able to change that once, but he knew he didn't have that kind of clout now.

He forced himself to work, reading over his students' notes on the dog they had in clinic at the moment. Vitals were good. The leg was healing. He flipped the page back, skimming the latest X-rays of the fracture. If they kept on track, they'd be able to send him home before Christmas, which meant Hunter might be patient-free for the holidays.

The windowpane rattled as thunder hit—closer now. A blinding flash of lightning flooded the room with white light.

"Hunter?" Jo's voice was soft.

"It's just a storm. Go back to sleep, Jo." He kept his voice low, watching her.

She rolled over, burrowing into the blanket. But the next clap of thunder had her on her feet. He saw her grab her head, leaning against the edge of the sofa.

"Still hurting?" He'd do just about anything to make her feel better. "Want me to take you home?"

She nodded, but then the sky seemed to open up. Sheets of rain dumped onto the tin roof, followed by a show of flashing lightning and roaring thunder. She looked out the window and shook her head.

He smiled. "Still afraid of storms? And you live in Washington?"

"Yes. Yes, I am." She tried to give him a look, one that showed him how capable and tough she was. But the thunder sent her from the couch to his side. "It doesn't storm like this there. It just rains…a lot."

He hesitated only briefly before slipping one hand around her waist. His heart picked up and he waited, but she was too focused on what was happening outside to notice his touch. She was warm—he could feel that through the thin fabric of her shirt. He tugged, pulling her into his lap gently, hungrily. When she sat, her body pressed against him, he couldn't stop the tremor that racked his body.

"I forgot how violent storms get here," she whispered.

He couldn't answer. She was in his arms, in his lap. She felt just the same, warm and soft in all the right places. He stared at her face, rediscovering the shape of her. He used to hold her like this for hours. Sitting, talking, kissing and being happy. How could so much time have passed? She hadn't changed, and neither had his feelings.

"Is it… Are we safe?" she asked, glancing at him. And then she realized she was in his lap, his arms were around her. Her eyes went round. Surprised. Startled. Pleased? He couldn't tell.

He swallowed. "Inside we're safe. We should probably try to wait it out, though, instead of taking you back."

She nodded, her eyes never leaving his. He expected her to tense, to pull away from him. But she seemed just as wrapped up in him as he was in her. Her breath hitched, her gaze falling to his lips. He knew an invitation when he saw one.

He bent his head, moving close, slowly. She watched him, her breathing picking up. Did she know how she affected him? He didn't want to push her, to lose her. Everything he wanted was right here, in his arms.

And then she pulled away. "We can't do this, Hunter." Her voice was husky and not at all convincing.

"Sure we can."

"No, we can't." She pushed halfheartedly against his chest. But her fingers gripped his shirt.

He knew his need for her was there, on display, but he didn't care. He wanted her, he'd never stopped. To him, she was still his. "Why?" he asked.

Something about that question pushed Jo over

the edge. She was out of his lap in no time, staring down at him with blazing eyes and an angry twist to her mouth. "Why?"

He looked up at her, confused. "You want me. At least, I think you do. And I know I want you."

She froze, her hands fisting at her sides. "You do?"

"Hell, yes." He stood as he spoke, his hands resting on her shoulders.

She shook her head, but she was staring at his mouth. "No. Hunter." He saw her indecision, her frustration. "What we *want* has nothing to do with what's *right*."

He heard "what we want" and pulled her against him. His hands cupped her face, his thumb brushing across her lower lip. He felt her shudder, saw her lips part, before she stiffened. Why was she fighting? He'd missed this, the feel of her in his arms, the wholeness he felt deep in his bones. How could he tell her, make her understand? His throat tightened as he stared at her, willing her to know what was in his heart.

Her chin quivered. "Hunter," she whispered, her voice hitching. "I can't do this to Eli. To Amy."

Hunter's chest grew cold. "Amy?"

She winced when he said the name. "Yes, A-Amy." She pushed away from him, wrapping her arms around her waist.

He didn't know what to say to that. He'd hoped that there might be some way for them to come to terms with what had happened, what he'd done. He'd never expected her to take him back, but he'd hoped she'd forgive him. She was here, but somehow Amy was still between them.

His phone rang, but neither of them moved. It could wait. "Jo—"

It rang again.

"Aren't you going to get that?" she murmured, her eyes cold.

"I'd rather talk to you."

"There's nothing to talk about." She shook her head, her anger building. "Nothing. I shouldn't be here. This—" she pointed frantically back and forth between the two of them "—is wrong."

Her words hurt. "Wrong?" He swallowed. "How can you—"

"How can I? You promised me, remember? I'm not going to let you break my heart again, Hunter. Do us both a favor and leave me the hell alone." She grabbed the phone. "Hold on," she said into the phone before tossing it to him.

He caught it, Fisher's voice reaching him. "Hunter? Hunter?"

"Yes?" he spoke into the phone, keeping his gaze locked with Jo.

"Fence is down in the far pens." Fisher laughed. "You're going to have to get Jo back into bed later on."

She crossed her arms over her chest, scowling at him. She looked so damn vulnerable, wounded somehow. But then she picked up her purse and headed to the door.

He stepped forward, blocking her path, fear rising. "Jo, hold on—"

Jo shook her head, pushing around him. "I don't want to hold on, Hunter. I don't want this. I don't want you. Not anymore." She ran out into the rain and climbed into her car.

"Hunter?" Fisher sounded stunned. "You there? You okay? Shit, I'm sorry—"

He cleared his throat, swallowing the lump to say, "On my way." He watched her car back up, then turn around, disappearing into the driving rain and darkness.

Chapter Three

Josie straightened the remaining pastries and sat in the little chair in the doorway between the kitchen and the bakery. Sprinkles lay on her back, her fuzzy white stomach bared as she slept soundly. Josie envied the dog—she could use a nap. She glanced at the clock. It was almost two, closing time.

But today she had to help with the gingerbread, mountains and mountains of it. Her dad's fall had put the gingerbread dough-making behind. Somehow, she had to make eighty gallon tubs of cookie dough in the next forty-eight hours. The Gingerbread Village was a huge part of the Stonewall Crossing's Christmas on the Square celebration. Most families made a gingerbread house to display. Some made them look like their own home, others followed the theme for the year. This year's theme, which Josie thought left a lot of room for interpretation, was Images of Christmas.

The phone rang and she answered it, pen and notepad at the ready.

"Pop's Bakery. This is Josie. How can I help you?"

"Hey, Miss…Jo…Josie. It's Eli Boone." He paused. "I have the plans for the float. Can I come by and show it to you?"

She smiled. "Sure, Eli. But I'll warn you. You might just end up elbow deep in gingerbread dough when you get here."

"O-okay." He sounded uncertain. "Can I bring someone with me?"

"Can they hold a mixer?" Josie added. "Just kidding. Bring as many as you like."

He didn't laugh. "Yes, ma'am. Be there soon."

"Sounds good." And she hung up the phone.

Eli was a good kid. He was just like his father. Or how he used to be, anyway.

She didn't linger over thoughts of Hunter. Whatever memories she had of him were tarnished somehow. She'd been so young—they both had. He'd loved her with an unwavering strength. He'd been hers and she'd been his. It had been right and good and real. Losing him was like losing a part of her, the pain of which had faded to a steady hollow ache she still couldn't erase.

But maybe the Hunter she remembered had never existed. Maybe he'd cheated on her with Amy as eagerly as he'd been willing to cheat on Amy.

It scared her, how tempted she'd been.

But saying Amy's name had snapped her out of it and pissed her off. She'd been just mad enough to drive herself home. By the time she was home, her head was throbbing in time to the beat of the rain. She'd crawled into her bed in her wet clothes, angry, needy and confused.

She'd spent the past two days not thinking about him. It wasn't really working…

And now she was going to spend some quality time with his son.

The phone rang again. "Pop's Bakery."

"Got your voice message. I talked to our librarian and she wants you to come read to the kids next Friday." The voice on the end of the line was soft, tired.

"Why, good morning, Annabeth. I'm fine, thanks for calling. How are you?" Josie teased.

"Work is crazy, girl. I'm sorry." Annabeth sighed. "How are you?"

"Not half as tired as you sound."

Annabeth Upton had been Josie's only real girlfriend in high school. She'd been there through everything, from Hunter's betrayal to her mom's endless string of weddings and divorces. Josie had tried to return the favor when Annabeth lost her husband to a sniper in Afghanistan. But she didn't know how to ease the pain of losing the man you loved while having to be a coherent, positive single parent to a rambunctious boy.

"I won't lie. I'm ready for the break."

"I can't imagine why. Being an elementary school principal is one of the easiest jobs in the world."

Annabeth laughed. "R-right."

"Are you going to get a break? Heading to Greg's family this year?"

"No, not this year. His parents offered to take Cody for New Year's so I could do something." She snorted. "What the hell am I going to do? Alone? In Stonewall Crossing?"

"Whatever you want," Josie said.

"That's the thing. I have no idea." She sighed. "So, how's it going? I know you're spread thin, with your dad and the bakery and the gingerbread craziness. And Hunter—"

"Dad's being ornery, but that's why I'm here." Josie was quick to interrupt her. Not thinking about Hunter. Not talking about Hunter. "We're heading to the doctor on Monday, so we'll see what the verdict is."

"Ready to get out of here?"

"Not really." Leaving meant going back to an empty apartment. This would be her first holiday without Wes. She didn't blame him for leaving, but she was lonely.

"You sound surprised." Annabeth paused. "And I did notice your attempt to dodge the whole Hunter topic. Not very subtly, either, I might add."

"Okay, let's talk about him."

"Let's. Over wine and dinner?" She added, "You can call Lola to come over and keep your dad company."

"Lola?"

"Josie, get your head out of the clouds and look around you. Lola, from the beauty shop two stores down the street. She's sweet on Carl."

Josie was surprised, in a good way. "And Dad?"

"I have no idea. Your dad rarely has a harsh

word for anyone. So, call her so your dad can get a love life. Then we can have dinner and drinks and talk about our nonexistent love lives."

"Deal." She'd call Lola right away.

"Good. Oh, hold on." There was a pause. "Will next Friday's story time work?"

"Yes, ma'am, Mrs. Upton. I'll put it on my calendar."

"Thanks. Gotta go. Duty calls… Kindergarteners, noses and peas… Bye."

"Bye." Josie laughed, but the phone was already dead.

She stared out over the freshly mopped wooden floors, her gaze drifting around the bakery. Lola Worley was a blue-haired sweetie. And, come to think of it, Lola had enjoyed a cup of tea and a small bear claw every morning since Josie had arrived in Stonewall Crossing five days before.

She packed up a plate of pastries, patted the flour from her clothes and walked quickly down the sidewalk to the Lady's Parlor. It was cold out, surprisingly cold, but she'd been too preoccupied to think of grabbing her sweater. She pushed through the door, the smell of acetone and bleach stinging her nose. Four heads turned to look at her.

"Joselyn Stephens?" Lola stepped forward. "What a surprise."

"Afternoon, Miss Worley. I thought I'd bring by some pastries for your patrons."

"Don't that just beat all?" Lola took the pastries, smiling. "What can I do for you, sugar? A haircut? Polish for your nails?"

Josie looked at her nonexistent nails before shoving her hands in her pockets. "I was wondering if you could help me."

Lola set the plate on the counter. "Sure thing, sugar. With what?"

"My dad. He's a little stubborn."

"Just a little." Lola Worley turned a very fetching shade of pink.

"Annabeth and I would like to go out this evening. Would you be willing to come over, take care of him? I won't be late."

Lola took in a deep breath. "I'd be happy to."
Josie could tell that was an understatement.
"Anything else?"

"Well—"

"Go on, sugar. You're among family here."
Lola patted her arm.

Josie looked around the beauty parlor, where chatter and laughter filled the air. "I'm swimming in all the gingerbread. Dad won't sit so—"

"I've got a half-dozen grandsons I'll send down this evening."

"Lola, you're an angel." Josie nodded. "I'll return the favor, if ever I can."

"Aw, now, I don't know about that, sugar. I'll see you about six?" Lola asked.

"Yes. And thank you." She hugged the woman before dashing out of the parlor and back to the bakery. Eli was waiting outside with a red-haired girl.

"You can go in. I know its cold out here." She held the door open for them.

Eli nodded at her. "Hey."

"Hi, I'm Dara. Nice to meet you, Miss Stephens," Dara gushed.

"You, too, Dara." She beamed at the girl, then at Eli. Eli didn't smile back. "Can't wait to see the sketches." She waved them back behind the counter.

Eli stood between the two of them and spread open a large piece of drafting paper. A chair sat in the middle of the float, flanked by two supersize books.

"These will have the covers for *Floppy Ears* and *34*," Eli pointed out. "Mrs. Upton said she wants to get the little brothers and sisters of the Future Farmers of America kids to ride on the float with you. Make it like you're reading to them."

Josie nodded. "And these?" She pointed to two blob-like shapes.

"One will be a cow and one will be a rabbit," Dara said. "We're going to make them out of garland and wrap them with lights. You know, those topiary things?"

"It looks great." Josie was impressed. "And a lot of work."

"It was Eli's idea." Something in Dara's tone made Josie look at the girl.

"It's a great idea," Josie said. She saw Dara cast a timid glance Eli's way, saw Eli's red cheeks. Just when Eli looked at Dara, the girl looked back at the drawing.

The bell over the door rang.

"Hey, Josie-girl." Fisher was all smiles. "How's it going?"

"Gingerbread madness has begun." She grinned. "Nice of you to stop by to help."

"I'll help eat my fair share. It sure smells good." Fisher sniffed for emphasis.

"Tastes pretty good, too." Josie offered the three of them a gingerbread man.

"Damn good," Fisher agreed, eating the cookie in two bites. "You good with the plans?"

She nodded. "Since I'm not building it, yes. Looks great."

Dara's phone rang so she walked outside to take the call, and Eli followed.

"They're adorable," she said to Fisher.

"Eli's too young for a girlfriend," Fisher argued. "He's just a kid."

"I don't think they're talking marriage, Fisher." She offered him another cookie. "How've you been?"

"I'm good, real good. Nothing like living your dream while being seriously good-looking, you know?"

She giggled. "You're incredible."

"I've heard that before." He winked at her.

She kept laughing. "Behave."

"Not in my nature," he countered.

"Fisher," she wheezed. "You're going to make me have an asthma attack."

He chuckled. "Never done that to a woman before."

She shook her head. Fisher had always been funny. Once she was able to breathe and talk, she tried again. "I'm really impressed by the ranch. Looks like the family has been working hard."

"Mom and Dad set the bar pretty high. And Hunter. He's going to reach that bar, and then some. Archer's a genius, really taking the whole refuge thing to the next level. I mean, we're getting eleven abused horses—that's a lot. But he'll figure it out." He shook his head. "Now, Ryder's still more interested in cars and petite blondes than anything else, but he works hard when we need him."

"How's Renata?" Josie had always felt for Renata, Fisher's twin sister. She couldn't imagine having four brothers and Teddy Boone for a father.

"Renata's working for the chamber of commerce. Does their PR and events and stuff."

"Sounds like the Boones still own Stonewall Crossing."

"Can't help it if our people were competitive from the start. We don't own it, exactly."

"No? Just most of it?" She argued, "If I remember the little tour I took when I first moved in with dad, they said the town was named Stone-wall Crossing because your great-grandfather put up stone walls to line his property."

"Great-great-grandfather. Man is a territorial animal, Josie. Those walls are a surefire way to let people know where not to trespass." Fisher shrugged.

"How is your father?" She'd missed him. Teddy Boone was a great barrel-chested man who let everyone know when he entered a room.

"Fine. He lives in the Lodge. He still misses Mom a lot. Think leading guests to check out the flowers when the hills are blooming, or hike, or bird-watch keeps him busy. In the hotter months, he's with the aunts in Montana. He's here now, so stop by and say hi. He'd love that."

She nodded. "He must be so proud of every-thing you have accomplished."

"Hunter started it, getting all successful. We couldn't let him show us up, you know?" He swiped another gingerbread cookie. "That

Boone competitive streak. You know Hunter. Hell, I think you know Hunter best of all." His expression turned serious—as serious as Fisher ever got.

"No, not really."

"Aw, come on, Josie. That's not true—"

"Years ago, maybe." She put the sample plate behind the counter and began to wipe down the counter. "Why does everyone keep talking about the past?"

"What's got you so worked up?"

She shut the display case with a little more force than necessary. "Nothing."

"Right."

"Moving on." She shot him a look. "You dating anyone?"

He winked at her. "I'm flattered, but I don't think that would go over too well with my brother."

She hadn't meant to yell, but she did. "Why the hell would Hunter care if I dated anyone? He's married, remember?"

If she hadn't been yelling, she might have heard the bell over the door jingle. But she didn't. So Eli's angry words took her by complete surprise. "My mom divorced my dad when I was three."

Josie couldn't think. Or speak. Or breathe. The agony on Eli's face was unbearable. "I…I didn't know. I'm sorry, Eli," she finally managed.

"You should be," Eli bit out. "It's your fault she left."

"Eli," Fisher cut in.

Josie was reeling. "Eli, I…" She had no words. She knew nothing she said could make a difference.

Dara placed a hand on Eli's arm. "Walk me home?" Eli didn't look up as Dara led him from the bakery.

Her heart ached for him, truly ached for him. She knew how hard it was, growing up without a mother. If she'd been the cause of that… No, surely not. Hunter was a man of his word. He'd married Amy—he wouldn't have let it fall apart without a fight.

"What is all the yelling about?" Her father hobbled into the kitchen through the door that connected their home to the bakery. "I could hear you all the way in my room."

Josie watched Eli and Dara walk away. She saw the slump to Eli's shoulders, knew the anger and pain in his voice.

"How the hell did you not know he's single?" Fisher asked, stunned.

"What are we talking about?" her father asked.

"Hunter." Fisher reached around the counter for another gingerbread cookie.

"Oh." Her father sounded far too pleased, so she looked at him. "What?"

"What?" she echoed. "That's all you have to say?" *Hunter Boone is single.*

Her father's smile disappeared. "You told me if I ever mentioned him you'd never talk to me again. Guess I figured the more time the two of you spent together, you'd figure things out."

"Seriously, Josie?" Fisher shook his head, then ate another cookie.

"Every time I brought him up, you changed the subject. I got the point," her father continued.

"That was a long time ago." He hadn't mentioned Hunter or the rest of his family in years. Because she'd told him not to. Josie grabbed the plate and shoved it into a cabinet out of Fisher's reach. "I was young and hurt—"

"You're my baby girl. And I listened to you," her father interrupted. "I figured someday you'd find out that he was here, waiting for you."

Josie glared at her father. "Daddy, I know you love Hunter. But that's ancient history—"

"Maybe for you." Fisher's eyebrows went up.

Her father's voice was cautious. "Now, Fisher—"

Fisher leaned forward, staring into her eyes. "Ask me how many dates my brother's been on since Amy left."

She didn't want to know, did she? No. She didn't.

"Let's give her some time to get used to things, Fisher." Her father chuckled. "Her whole world just got flipped upside down."

She lied quickly, to herself and the two of them. "Nothing has changed. Nothing. I'm here to take care of you, Dad, not relive some teenage romance." She yanked the apron over her head and threw it on the back counter.

"Josie," Fisher groaned. "Come on now."

She held up her hand. "Stop. *Please.*" She paused. "I'm tired. I need a shower. I just hurt a boy that I'd never in a million years want to hurt. So, please, just stop."

Her father exchanged a quick look with Fisher before he sighed. "It's closing time, anyway."

"I'll lock up," Josie offered, looking pointedly at Fisher.

Fisher took the hint. "Eli will be all right. You okay?"

She nodded but wouldn't look at him.

Fisher left and Josie locked the door behind him. She took her father's arm, leading him back into the house.

"Should I have told you, Josie?" her father asked.

"No, Dad." She patted his hand. There was no way to go back. Thinking about what could have been, what might have happened, was pointless. "It doesn't matter. Now go sit, and I'll get you some water. Maybe a snack?"

Her father nodded, moving slowly to his recliner in the other room. She headed into the kitchen, grappling with too many emotions to understand. But a part of her—a part deeply buried inside—felt relief. He wasn't a cheater. He wasn't a liar. He had loved her. Maybe he still—

"Josie, bring the car around," her father yelled. "We gotta get Sprinkles to the hospital."

HUNTER'S CELL SCREEN lit up. *Amy.* He hadn't had enough coffee for this yet.

Tripod, the black three-legged cat that roamed the hospital, glared at the phone from his napping spot on the corner of Hunter's desk.

Hunter nodded in agreement. "I know the feeling."

Tripod yawned, stood and stretched, then

curled back up in a ball on the desk. Hunter stroked the cat's silky side, letting the animal's reverberating purr calm him before answering the phone.

"How's the sexiest man in the world?" Amy's drawl was light, teasing. "Wearing your tight jeans and your jump-me doctor coat?"

He'd learned not to bite to her teasing. "How are you, Amy?" He clicked the end of his pen a few more times.

"All business this morning? Guess it's hard to talk dirty at the office." She sighed. "I'd be better if I was there with Eli. And you."

"You coming through town?" He kept clicking the pen.

"I'm trying. You know I want to be there." She sighed again. "I'd never miss Christmas with my baby if I could help it." She paused, but he kept quiet. "But I've got a chance to ride in Vegas through New Year's. Big show, you know?"

Amy spent more time with the cowboys on

the rodeo circuit than riding in it, but all he said was, "I'll let you tell Eli."

She made that noise, that irritated, impatient sound she made when she wasn't getting her way. He remembered that noise all too well.

"Don't use that tone with me, Hunter Boone. I don't need your approval or your permission."

"I know." He tossed his pen onto his desk and leaned back in his chair, staring up at the white insulation tiles of the ceiling.

"Good. You don't know how hard it is, to live without the perfect parents and buckets of money just sitting around their big ol' fancy house." Her voice was shaking. "A gal's gotta eat, Hunter."

There it was. "How much do you need?"

"I don't need a handout," she snapped.

"You're Eli's mom, his family. It's not a hand-out. It's family taking care of family."

The phone was silent for a long time. "You don't miss me at all? Us?"

He didn't say, "No, Amy. I don't. I won't. Stop messing with our son and grow up." He'd learned not to have any expectations when it came to Amy—then there was no disappointment. But Eli was a boy—a boy wanting to believe the very best about his mother. Even if a lot of it wasn't true. And now his mother was missing Christmas with him…again.

It tore his heart out to see his boy hurting. He was used to buying a present and putting Amy's name on it, but he resented having to cover for her. It shouldn't be his job to maintain a relationship between his ex-wife and his son.

"Dr. Boone." Jason, one of his students, came running into his office. "Larry ate Hanna's hair scrunchie again."

"Hold on a sec, Amy?" He covered his phone. "Is Larry breathing okay?"

"Yes, sir. But he's coughing a little."

Hunter sat back, ran a hand over his face. Why Larry the emu liked eating hair scrunchies was a mystery. But they could be dangerous to the animal if they got stuck in his trachea. "Please ask Hanna to set up the ultrasound machine. I'll expect her to assist in fifteen minutes." Since he'd told Hanna several times to remove her hair accessories before she went into the pen, she would help him scan the bad-tempered bird and, if necessary, remove it from the bird's long neck.

"Yes, sir." Jason left.

"Still there?" he asked.

"I'm here, waiting. But I've got people waiting, too. I'll call our son tonight." And she hung up.

He was about to throw his cell phone against the wall when a soft "Dr. Boone" was followed by a knock on his office door.

He repressed an irritated sigh as one of the school deans entered. He stood, extending his hand to the older man. "Dr. Lee," he said. "Nice to see you."

"You, as well." Dr. Lee nodded, shaking his hand. "I hear you have a procedure in fifteen minutes, so I won't keep you. But I need your help. We have received a substantial donation from the Harper-McGee family—an in memoriam for their deceased son Nate."

Hunter nodded. The Harper-McGees were one of the school's most devoted supporters. The past five generations of Harper-McGees had earned their doctor of veterinary medicine degrees from UET's College of Veterinary Medicine. Nate would have carried on that tradition if he hadn't been killed in a car accident midsemester last spring.

"Part of the donation is to be used for a mural in the waiting room. His parents have a drawing he did when he was young. They want something like it to cover the wall over the admissions desk."

Hunter looked at the drawing Dr. Lee offered him, then back at the older man. "I'm not sure—"

"Dr. Hardy told me you're very close with the local artist Joselyn Stephens. That she's visiting right now. Dr. and Mrs. Harper-McGee were delighted. They hoped you'd convince her to consider their commission."

Hunter blinked. "I don't know Miss Stephens

all that well. But I do see her father now and then." He didn't know if he could see her again, to talk business or otherwise. Her angry words were a hot band around his heart.

"Perhaps you could ask her to contact me, then? Their donation is incredibly generous, Dr. Boone. I'd like to be as accommodating as possible, you understand?" Dr. Lee nodded at the drawing. "These are for Miss Stephens." He placed a sealed envelope on top of the sketch. "If she has any questions, I'm sure there's contact information inside."

Hunter stared at Joselyn's name on the envelope. "I'll get it to her."

"Thank you, Dr. Boone." Dr. Lee nodded. "Good luck with Larry."

Hunter smiled. "Good training opportunity."

The older man paused at the door. "How's the pharaoh hound?"

Hunter ran a hand over his head. "Bad-tempered. Stubborn. And spoiled." But the owners were willing to keep spending thousands of dollars on their rare breed, so until puppies were a guarantee, the damn dog was Hunter's problem.

"Any animal that needs help procreating has a right to be all of those things." Dr. Lee chuckled.

"Never thought about it that way," Hunter agreed. "We can only hope the procedure works this time."

Hunter thought letting Tut have some fun the old-fashioned way might sort out his quick temper. But the owners were determined, and footing the bill, so petri dishes, test tubes and no hanky-panky were all Tut had to look forward to.

"Poor Tut. We shall hope for the best. I do hope Larry behaves for you." Dr. Lee stopped at the door. "If I don't see you before the holiday, enjoy your break."

"Thank you. You, too." No sooner had Dr. Lee left than Hunter's office phone rang. He tried not to snap as he answered, "Dr. Boone."

"Dr. Boone, we're checking in Sprinkles, Mr. Stephens's rat terrier."

He could pass the dog off to another resident. Maybe he should. But Carl was recovering right now. And Jo— "On my way." It took him two minutes to leave the administration wing, pass the massive lecture halls and labs, and enter the teaching clinic.

The first thing Hunter saw was Josie, her arm around her father. Her hair had slipped free from the clip on her head, falling down her back in thick reddish-brown curls. Her shirt was covered in a fine coating of flour; two more streaks ran across her forehead and into her hairline. He smiled at the flour handprint on her hip.

Her words rang in his ears, branding his heart. But seeing her worried and disheveled only reminded him that she was hurting, too. This time, right now, he could make it better.

She saw him then, her gray eyes widening before everything about her relaxed. "He's here, Dad. It'll be okay."

Damn, she looked beautiful. "Hi."

Carl was clutching a trembling Sprinkles to his chest. "Hunter, I didn't know if you were working the clinic today—"

"You think I'd let anyone else take care of Sprinkles?" Hunter patted the dog's head, looking into the small canine's brown eyes. He glanced at the desk clerk. "Call Dr. Archer in to assist with Larry. Jason and Hanna should have him prepped and ready to go."

"Yes, Dr. Boone. Room four is open," she added.

He nodded, assessing the situation. Yes, Sprinkles was sick, but Carl was clearly worn-out. "How about I carry Sprinkles?" Hunter took the dog. "Follow me."

He placed his hand over the dog's chest, counting the beats per minute. One thirty-six. Nothing irregular. Breathing was a little labored, but Sprinkles didn't like riding in the car, so that was just as likely to cause her panting as anything. Once they were in the exam room, he put

Sprinkles on the metal exam table and looked at Carl. "What happened?"

"Dad, please sit." Jo pulled one of the chairs closer to the table.

"I don't know." Carl sat in the chair, resting his hand on the dog's head. "I just don't know. Sprinkles and I were watching a John Wayne flick, a good one. Then Josie and Fisher were yelling in the bakery, so I left to see what they were going on about. Sprinkles was in my chair. I came back and she's lying on the floor, acting like this." He pointed at Sprinkles for emphasis. The dog was definitely not her normal, bouncing, yapping self.

Hunter put the earpieces of his stethoscope in and listened to Sprinkles's stomach. "Did she eat anything?"

"Her food," Carl answered. "You give her anything, Josie?"

Hunter looked at Jo and froze. She was staring at him, intently. In the depths of her silver gaze he saw something that made him ache. What was going on inside that head of hers?

"Josie?" Carl repeated, making Jo jump and reminding Hunter he had a job to do.

"No, I didn't." Her hand rested on her father's shoulder. "You've told me a dozen times she's on a special diet."

Carl patted his daughter's hand.

Hunter focused on the dog. "Could she have gotten into something?"

"She gets into everything," Carl admitted.

"I've had to chase her out of my suitcase every morning." Jo smiled.

"She eat something bad? Josie, you have perfume or something that could make her sick?"

"No, Dad. Besides, if she'd drunk my perfume, she'd smell better." Jo's voice was teasing.

"That's not funny, Joselyn Marie."

Like hell it isn't. Hunter winked at Jo.

He saw the splash of color on her cheeks, the way she blinked and looked at her father. "Sorry, Dad." She bent, pressing a kiss to Carl's temple.

"I don't think we need to get too worried just yet," Hunter said as Sprinkles stood up. Her little stomach tensed and she vomited a glob of clear gelatinous fluid onto the metal exam table.

"Sprinkles," Carl groaned.

"Jo?" Hunter used a long exam swab to poke the goop. "You use any sort of face cream?"

"Yes. Anti-wrinkle gel."

Hunter stood back and grinned. "I'd check the container when you get home. Bet it's gone."

Carl glared up at Jo.

"Dad." Josie shook her head. "It was on the vanity counter, out of her reach."

"Sprinkles has always been a good jumper, if I remember," Hunter said. Sprinkles had belonged to old Mrs. Henry for three years before she'd decided a cat was less work for her. Hunter had offered to help find the dog a home. Carl and Sprinkles had taken one look at each other and clicked.

Carl nodded. "Guess I need to put on some of those baby locks to keep her out of things."

Sprinkles vomited again, shaking.

Hunter watched. "Might be best if we keep her here—"

"Nope." Carl shook his head. "I'll keep an eye on her."

Hunter glanced at Jo, who shrugged at him. "Dad—"

"No." Carl wasn't taking no for an answer. "She'll be happier at home. We can keep her in her kennel."

"You need to keep her hydrated," Hunter said.

"Anything else?" Carl asked.

"Don't feed her." Hunter glanced between the two of them. He couldn't help it if his attention lingered on Jo. "Not today, anyway. We'll see how she is tomorrow."

"Okay," she said, her gaze meeting his. "Maybe you could swing by and check on her later?"

Hunter stared at her then. He was more than willing to make a house call for Sprinkles. But he'd expected Carl to make the suggestion, not

Jo, not after their exchange the other night. Did he dare smile at her? He wanted to.

"Hey, now, that's an idea." Carl nodded.

"If you're free?" She seemed uncertain, hesitant.

Now he really wanted to know what was going on in that beautiful, stubborn head of hers. "I'll stop by later." He'd leave work now if he thought it would mean more time with her. "And I'll install the baby locks, if you have them for me."

"Fine, but if we're putting you to work, we're feeding you." Carl stroked the dog's head. Sprinkles whimpered. "Come here." Carl pulled the little dog close.

"Carl," Hunter cautioned. "At least let me get you a towel. Things are gonna get messy real fast."

He saw Jo's nose wrinkle and laughed.

Carl rubbed Sprinkles's head. "See there, it's gonna be fine, little girl."

When Jo looked at him, her gray gaze was searching. She drew in an unsteady breath and mouthed, "Thank you." He couldn't stop staring at her then. He didn't want to.

The intercom buzzed. "Dr. Boone, you're needed in OR 1, please."

"On my way. Please ask Janette to bring in some diapers and a towel for the Stephenses."

"Yes, sir." The intercom went quiet.

"Thank you, Hunter." Carl shook his hand.

"Hunter, if...if you can't make it tonight—" Jo seemed nervous, flustered.

"I'll be there," he promised before leaving the room.

Chapter Four

"Something smells good," Carl called from his recliner.

"If you stay there, I might just bring you a taste," Josie yelled back. "You get up and you're having a peanut butter sandwich."

"I'm sitting, I'm sitting," her father grumbled.

"How's Sprinkles?" She finished basting the roast and slid it back into the oven.

"She's sleeping again," he answered her. "Poor little thing."

Josie shook her head. Better sleeping than needing another cleanup.

She dumped the homemade rolls into a basket and covered them with a fresh linen kitchen towel. Next she boiled some water and put in some tea bags to steep. Once Dad had lain down for his nap and Sprinkles was in a fresh diaper, she'd hurried to the small grocery store for food. She didn't know who was coming tonight. Dad, Lola and Hunter. Possibly Eli, or the whole Boone clan. A nice roast, complete with potatoes, carrots and fresh onions, had been simmering for the past couple of hours.

"You got the baby locks?" he called.

"Yes, Dad."

"You sure you have to go out tonight?" Her father kept up the semi-screamed conversation.

Yes, she was sure. What had she been thinking—inviting him over for dinner? She couldn't risk spending more time with Hunter. She wanted to, a lot, but there was no point. Hunter wasn't married—he could date anyone he wanted. *Except* her.

Eli hated her. As far as he was concerned, she was the cause of his parents' divorce. And there was no way to change that. If there was one thing life had taught her, it was that nothing should come between a parent and child. How many times had her mother missed her art exhibitions or play performances while dating or divorcing one of her husbands? Each and every time Josie was forgotten. It didn't matter that she'd eventually be drawn into her mother's new family, because that was temporary, too. Love and trust were the two things she didn't have a lot of experience with while growing up.

She wouldn't threaten the bond he and Hunter shared. In some pretty perfect world, she and Hunter might have been able to make it work. But that wasn't real life. Eli needed his father and Hunter needed his son. So, even though everything had changed, nothing had changed. Avoiding Hunter, trying to convince Eli she had no plans for his father, was all she could do until it was time to move to New Mexico—if she took the job. She'd been a vagabond for almost three years now, six months here, four months there.

Signing on with the Art Institute in New Mexico would be a huge change.

She wasn't meant for love or marriage or relationships—she was too much like her mother.

Sprinkles croaked a bark, announcing their company's arrival.

"Come on in," her father called.

"Evening, Carl." She heard Hunter's voice and smiled. "What's cooking? My mouth is watering."

"Josie's been in there slaving away." She heard her father laugh. "Think she still feels guilty for poisoning Sprinkles."

"Dad!" She rubbed her hands on the front of her apron and walked into the living room.

Hunter, Eli and Dad were waiting. Her father and Hunter were grinning. Eli wasn't.

"He was funnin' you, Jo." Hunter shook his head, a bouquet of flowers in his hand.

"You brought flowers for Sprinkles?" her father asked. "Now, doesn't that beat all?" He winked at Josie. "Go get a vase, will you, Josie?

We can put the flowers on the mantel there, so Sprinkles can see them."

She shot her father a look. Was he teasing? "Sure." She turned, heading back into the kitchen.

"I didn't know I was buying Sprinkles flowers." Hunter was behind her.

She spun around. "Oh?" He was so tall, so close, so mind-blowingly gorgeous. She stepped back, her hip bouncing against the corner of the kitchen counter.

"I'm a devoted vet and all, but you gotta draw the line somewhere." His eyes crinkled as he smiled.

"So the flowers were for Dad," she teased, filling up a cut-glass vase. She took the blooms, clipping the ends off.

"I don't make a habit of buying flowers for animals or old men."

She glanced at him, arranging the flowers. "Nice to know Dad's special, then. Makes sense to me."

They stared at each other for a long time. She wasn't sure what to say or do. He was just standing there. Taking up the air in the room. Staring at her, a crooked grin on his face.

"Sprinkles is awake," her dad announced, followed by the sound of the dog throwing up.

Hunter laughed. "How's it going?"

"A lot of that." She nodded in the direction of the living room. "Dad's been watching her like a hawk."

"Hello?" Lola's voice was singsongy. "How are both our patients?"

Josie relaxed.

"Evening, Miss Worley. Can I get that for you?" Eli entered the kitchen carrying a cake plate. Lola followed close behind. She gave everyone a quick hug.

"Mmm, something smells good." Lola peeked in the stove. "You made fresh rolls, too? What a good little wife you'd make." She patted Josie's cheek. "You go on and have fun tonight. Me and the boys here will keep your dad in line."

Hunter looked at her. "You're going out?"

She nodded.

"A well-deserved night out." Lola smiled. "Just point me in the direction of the plates."

Josie showed Lola around the kitchen and handed off her apron before joining her father in the living room.

"Did you shave?" Josie asked her father. She realized he hadn't been wearing the plaid button-down shirt an hour ago. His hair had been a little less groomed, too. She leaned forward to kiss him on the cheek. "Aftershave, too."

Her father turned an adorable shade of red.

She stood, hands on hips. "Promise me you'll behave. No showing off for Miss Lola. Not tonight, anyway."

"Joselyn Marie." Her father scowled up at her.

"Don't Joselyn Marie me." She glanced behind her to see Hunter coming from the kitchen, no Eli or Lola in tow. "Thanks for stopping by, Hunter."

He nodded, his smile tight, eyes burning. Was he mad?

"Need my purse," she murmured, hurrying into her room. She ran her fingers through her hair, put on some lip gloss and earrings, and checked her reflection. She grabbed her purse and headed out, dropping another kiss on her father's head and calling out, "Thanks again, Lola."

She left through the bakery, catching the door before it slammed. She fumbled with her keys.

"You don't really have to lock up out here," Hunter said.

She spun around, dropping the keys. "Habit," she managed. "Did I get the right baby locks?"

He bent, picking up her keys. He nodded at the toolbox on the porch, then looked at her. The heat in his eyes, the hunger, stole the air from her lungs.

"You need anything? Supplies?" she murmured as his eyes slowly explored the details of her face.

He shook his head, stepping closer and offering her the keys.

She took them, the brush of his fingers against hers stirring a tantalizing awareness along her skin. It wasn't fair, that he affected her like that. One little touch and she shivered. "It's cold," she lied.

His eyebrow arched.

She scowled at him. "Night." She forced herself to take one step, then another, and another.

"Have a good time tonight, Jo." His voice was husky.

"Thanks." She didn't look back as she headed down the sidewalk to the pool hall on the far side of the square.

"So he's at your dad's house, cleaning up dog throw-up and putting up baby locks, and you're here with me?" Annabeth took a long swig of her bottle of beer. "What's wrong with this picture?"

Josie finished off her beer. "Absolutely nothing."

Annabeth groaned. "You have a warm-blooded

man waiting and willing and you're not tossing his butt into your bed?"

Josie shot Annabeth a look. "Because I'm getting drunk with you."

"Then let's go."

"I can't." Josie shook her head, peeling the label off the beer.

"You can, Josie." Annabeth took a deep breath. "I'm going to say something really harsh here, okay?"

Josie looked at her. "Um, no, thank you."

"Tough. You're being ridiculous." She shook her head, blinking back the tears in her eyes. "Don't you get it? I'd give anything to have someone to go home to. You're choosing to be alone when you have this amazing, loyal man—"

"Annabeth." She shook her head. "I'm sorry. I am."

Annabeth patted her hand. "What do you want? Do you know?"

"To get Dad on his feet again—"

Annabeth shook her head. "*You?* What do you *want*?"

"I'm not sure." She swallowed, then leaned forward. "I'm scared. Okay?"

"Please don't start with that I'm-my-mom crap, okay?"

"Eli hates me." And it killed her.

"But Hunter doesn't." Annabeth's eyebrows went up. "We went out once, did you know that? We talked about you the whole time. He's kept up with you, proud of you." She shook her head. "Whatever. Enough about love and your need to throw it away. I want a man. Can you find me one?"

Josie laughed. "No. Don't have a lot of single men in my contacts list."

"Well, that gorgeous Ryder Boone is staring at us. I'm hoping he's checking me out and not you. That wouldn't be fair."

Josie glanced across the room. Sitting at the bar was a way-too-good-looking, smoldering-dark-and-dangerous type watching them.

"He looks annoyed." Josie tipped her beer back but realized it was empty. "So he's probably looking at me."

Annabeth rolled her eyes. "Oh, please. You don't annoy Hunter."

"You're right. *Annoy* isn't the right word."

"Arouse? Turn on?" Annabeth teased. "He just wants to jump your bones and make lots of babies with you."

"He does not," Josie argued, laughing. "Stop."

"What? What's wrong with intimacy? Seriously, Josie, you can't tell me you don't miss sex."

Josie leaned forward. "I didn't say I didn't, but—"

"So do it, have sex. Forget about the whole emotional baggage and focus on lots of good old wear-you-out, leave-you-smiling, rock-your-world, wake-your-neighbors sex."

"I'll drink to that." Ryder appeared, putting new beers on the table in front of them and making them both jump.

Josie stared at him. "God, Ryder, you're all grown-up—"

"And hot," Annabeth added. "I said that out loud, didn't I?"

Ryder looked at Annabeth, his heavy-lidded pale blue eyes smoldering. "I'll drink to that, too." He tipped his longneck, clinking it with Annabeth's.

"Please." Annabeth giggled, then rolled her eyes.

"Good to see you, Josie." Ryder was looking at her again. "Thought I'd get you ladies another round before heading out."

"Oh," Josie said. "Well, thanks for the beer."

"Thanks for the laugh." He smiled at her. "And have fun." He glanced at Annabeth. "You've got my number." He nodded at them both and made his way out of Shots.

Once he was gone, they both burst out laughing.

"I know I don't have the best field record at

dating, but I think that was a not-so-subtle cue for you to call the bad-boy Boone."

Josie couldn't help but notice the very *thoughtful* way Annabeth watched Ryder Boone climb on his motorcycle.

HUNTER SAT ON one of the rocking chairs on the front porch. He should go. Everything was done.

Sprinkles was doing better, but the diapers weren't ready to come off. The baby locks were installed and his tools packed away. While he'd worked on that, Eli and Lola had made a fridge full of gingerbread dough. Once Lola had retreated to a recliner to knit, he'd called Fisher to take Eli home. Lola dozed in the living room with Carl, so he managed to make a few more batches of gingerbread. Then cleaned up the kitchen.

When Lola walked out, she smiled down at him and patted his arm. "She's a good girl."

He didn't have a thing to say to that. He couldn't deny he was waiting around for Jo. He was.

"Walk an old lady home?" she asked.

He helped her into her coat and took her arm.

"Look at that moon." Lola pointed up at the low-hanging full moon. "Isn't it lovely?"

"Yes, ma'am." It was a gorgeous night. And there was nothing quite like seeing the town square and courthouse all lit up with Christmas lights. All the trees surrounding the courthouse were wrapped with thousands and thousands of lights. Even to his eye, it looked magical. "I love this time of year."

"Me, too, Hunter." She peered up at him. "What do you want for Christmas this year?"

He laughed, taking her keys and unlocking her door. "I'm too old for that, Miss Lola."

"Nonsense, Hunter. You're never too old for wishing. I've got one or two things on my list, but I'm not telling." She patted his arm again. "Thanks for the walk."

"Thanks for all your work."

"Josie needed a night out." Lola smiled. "Guess it's no secret I'm fond of that Carl Stephens." She waved, pulling her door shut.

Hunter set off back down the street to the bakery when he saw Josie. She lay on her back, sprawled out on the lawn of the courthouse. He didn't think—he ran. When he reached her side, he dropped to his knees.

She looked surprised. "Hunter?"

"What the hell are you doing, Jo?" he asked, his panic quickly replaced by irritation.

"I'm looking at the lights. All the colors. It's like a giant Christmas kaleidoscope." She patted the grass beside her. "Lie down, you'll see what I mean."

He shook his head but couldn't deny the smile tugging at his lips. "Are you drunk?"

"Maybe. A little." She giggled.

"It's forty degrees. Too cold for relaxing outside," he argued. "Where's your coat?"

She sighed. "Are you going to lie down or not? You're blocking part of my view."

He stared down at her. Her cheeks were red, her breath coming in puffs from the crisp air. Beneath the thousands and thousands of lights, her hair seemed to glow a warm and inviting red. She seemed to glow, so alive, so soft. It took everything he had not to touch her.

Instead, he flopped down on his back at her side.

"It's cold," he said.

"Hush. Open your eyes and stare straight up." Her voice was soft, almost a whisper. "See how the colored strands on the street shops bleed in around the edges of your vision?"

He stared up.

"Can you see it?" she asked, her hand nudging his.

Her fingers were icy cold, so he took her hand in his. He didn't look at her or acknowledge that his heart was thumping. He held her hand and stared at the lights. And the colors seemed to bloom around the edges. "I see it."

Her hand squeezed his. "Isn't it amazing?"

"Yeah."

They were silent for a while. Nothing but the sound of the wind through the trees, the slight clicking of the bouncing strands of lights. He could think of nothing sweeter than staying right here, touching her. But each gust of cold made it harder and harder for him to ignore she wasn't wearing a jacket. And it was only getting colder.

"Jo?" he whispered.

"Hmm?"

He turned his head and smiled. Her eyes were shut. Long lashes rested against her smooth skin. Her mouth was parted slightly, releasing a regular cloud of breath into the chilly night. "You still looking at the lights?"

Her eyes popped open. She blinked, then turned to face him.

He reached up, smoothing a curl from her face. "It's late."

She nodded, her hand tightening on his.

"Can I walk you home?" he asked.

She nodded again.

He stood, keeping her hand in his to pull her up. She didn't sway into him and he didn't pull her into his arms, no matter how much he wanted to. Instead, he took one of her hands, rubbing it briskly between his. "Your hands are ice cubes."

She was staring at their hands, but he saw her shiver. "Let's get you home." He led her to the sidewalk.

"It's snowing." She grabbed his arm with her free hand, tugging. "Look."

He looked up, watching the white flakes falling. "I'll be."

"I'll be?" She laughed. "What does that mean?"

He grinned at her. "No idea."

She kept laughing. Her heavy curls hung around her shoulders, her navy blue pullover clung to her curves, and she was laughing. With him. In the snow. And the vision took his breath away. He cleared his throat, tore his gaze away and led her across the street to the bakery. He didn't want to let go of her hand, of the tender camaraderie they'd found.

"Thanks for checking in on Sprinkles," she said, opening the door and standing aside.

He followed her in. "She'll be feeling better soon. Not tomorrow, though." He smiled. "Have fun?"

She nodded, looking at him with a sudden intensity. "Annabeth likes to remind me to stop and have some fun now and then."

"Sounds like good advice."

"You think so?" she asked, still assessing him. He nodded.

"Ryder thought so, too."

"Ryder was there?" He frowned.

"He bought me a beer."

"I bet he did." Women were drawn to Ryder like bees to honey. "Do I want to know what he considers fun?"

It had been a long time since he'd wanted to slug his brother, but the telltale blush that crept up Jo's neck said enough.

"He didn't really suggest anything. He just sort of agreed with Annabeth."

"What did she suggest?" He waited, beyond curious now.

She rubbed her hands together. "I think she worded it something like no-strings-attached, wake-your-neighbors sex."

He had no response for that. Part of him wanted to volunteer for the job. But the other part, his heart, knew there was no way he could ever have a no-strings-attached relationship with Jo. "And what do you think?"

"Well…I'm a little drunk." She grinned at him. "So it's probably something I should think about later. But it has potential, maybe."

He smiled. "Get some sleep, Jo." He opened the front door, glancing back at her.

"Sweet dreams, Hunter." Her sleepy-soft smile tempted him.

He swallowed, knowing damn well what his dreams would be. "You, too, Jo."

Chapter Five

"Pop's Bakery," Josie answered.

"Josie, it's Lola Worley."

Josie smiled. "Morning, Miss Lola. Staying warm?"

"You bet, sugar. Not liking the ice on the roads all that much, though." She paused. "I've got a favor. I know you're busy and all, but my grandson Tyler's in a fix."

Josie waved at the two older cowboys leaving the bakery. "What can I do?"

"Well, his uncle George was planning on coming in to talk to the kids about being a farrier for Career Night. But this ice has closed the roads and he can't get here."

"That's a shame."

"It is, it is. Especially since Tyler's getting extra credit for bringing in a speaker. He's having real trouble with math this year, let me tell you. Would you be willing to stand in? As an author, not a farrier."

She laughed. "That's a relief. I don't even know what a farrier is. When is it?"

"Tomorrow night. I know it's short notice and all—"

"I don't mind at all." She paused, thinking of her dad. "Would you be free to keep Dad company?"

Lola laughed. "I was hoping you'd ask."

"Lola—" Josie hesitated. "Why don't you just tell my dad you're sweet on him?"

"Josie!" Lola was laughing harder now. "I'm not going to do everything for the old coot."

"When you put it that way," Josie conceded.

"It starts at six. I'll be over at five-thirty?"

"Okay."

"I'll see you tomorrow night. Don't you worry

about feeding me, either. I make a chicken pot-pie your daddy just adores. Bye now."

Josie was still smiling when she hung up the phone.

"Any more gingerbread?" Josie looked up into the face of Teddy Boone. He had pale blue eyes framed by thick brown lashes. And when he smiled, as he was doing now, he had a wealth of fine lines to emphasize his good nature.

Josie was rooted to the spot.

"You better get over here and hug me, girl." Teddy waved her forward.

Josie ran around the counter and into the man's waiting arms. "Hi, Teddy."

"Hi, yourself." He held Josie back, inspecting her from head to toe. "You're a sight for sore eyes."

"And you look exactly the same."

He made a dismissive sound. "You look good, girl. Have time to sit and have a coffee? Or are you on the clock?"

Josie looked pointedly around the almost

empty dining room and shrugged. "Coffee sounds good."

Teddy sat while Josie put a few sugar cookies and gingerbread men on a plate. She poured two cups of hot coffee, added some eggnog and carried the whole tray to the table.

"You look like you're getting the hang of things here," Teddy said once Josie sat.

"It wasn't that long ago I worked here, remember?" She grinned. "If Miss Worley and Eli hadn't made so many tubs of dough, I'd be in big trouble."

"Glad Eli was a help." Teddy sipped his coffee. "He's a good boy. But he has his moments."

"Doesn't everyone?"

"Reminds me a lot of his daddy." Teddy nodded. "How's your dad?"

"His checkup yesterday went really well. He can start walking and doing a little."

"A little, huh? Good thing you're here." He took another sip, his gaze meeting Josie's. "Planning on staying?"

Josie shook her head.

"You're missed around here."

Josie stared at the sugar cookies on the plate. "There's a lot I've missed about Stonewall Crossing."

"Oh?" Teddy took a gingerbread cookie. "Hunter said you're working with the kids on their Christmas float."

"I haven't done a thing except tell them how nice the float looks." She smiled. "And it does."

"What else have you been up to? You've been moving around a bunch."

She nodded. "I think being restless is part of the artist thing. But I've been offered a job teaching art at my alma mater in New Mexico."

"Good for you." Teddy looked impressed. "I always knew you'd do good things. Like your books. Eli's copy of *34* has a frayed spine and dog-eared pages, we read it so much. It helped him through some tough times. Hunter, too, I think."

She stared at the cookies. Before Eli hated her,

he'd found comfort in her stories. And that was something. That he and Hunter shared them was all the better. The rush of heat in her cheeks assured her that, yes, she was blushing. Teddy's broad grin assured her that, yes, he'd noticed.

"Any more stories in the works?"

"Actually," Josie admitted, "Stonewall Crossing at Christmas deserves a story. Maybe." It had been a long time since she'd felt the pull of her sketch pad and writing journal, and she'd missed it. "But you're the first person I've told, so let's keep it a secret for now."

"Just me?" Teddy's brow furrowed. "No fella?"

"No. And that's okay." She shrugged. "I haven't found the right guy yet."

Teddy's smile was huge. "No?"

Josie couldn't help but smile back. "No."

"Well, I best be on my way. But I really do want to buy some gingerbread dough, please, ma'am. Something we can give our guests with hot chocolate. Been meaning to talk to your dad about letting me sell some out at the Lodge—good for business and all."

"Is that Teddy Boone?" her father called from the door that connected the house to the bakery.

"Hello, Carl." Teddy was all charm. "How's the hip, old man? Time to get you an electric scooter or is that walker working for you?"

"Kind of you to offer me yours, Teddy. But you can keep it for now. Come back in a month and I'll race ya, grandpa," her father shot back.

She wasn't sure if their back-and-forth jabs were adorable or pathetic, so she just stood there, hands on her hips, smiling.

"You're a lucky bastard, Carl. For not breaking your hip—" Teddy paused, smiling at Josie "—and for your sweet daughter."

"Don't I know it." Carl lifted two buckets of gingerbread onto the counter. "On the house. The least I can do after Hunter installed all those locks. According to Lola, he made a couple of batches, too."

"He did?" Josie asked, surprised. That's why

he'd stayed late? After tending to a sick dog, a grumpy old man and household repairs—he'd stayed late to make gingerbread. And walked her home without kissing her good-night. She swallowed.

"You would have known that if you hadn't gone out partying with Annabeth." Carl sighed.

Teddy frowned. "Now, Josie, you need to be careful. You don't want to go 'round attracting the wrong sort of fella's attention."

Josie looked at each of them, then burst out laughing. "I know. Stonewall Crossing is full of shady sorts," she teased. At the look on their faces she added, "I'll be careful."

"Thanks for the gingerbread, Carl. I'll make sure Hunter knows it's from you." Teddy winked at her. "So good to see you, girl. Carl, I want you and Josie to come have dinner with us. Holiday dinners are always nicer when you're surrounded by friends and family."

Before she could argue, her dad said, "We

couldn't impose on you, especially during the holidays, Teddy."

Thank you, Dad. No way she was up for a big Boone family dinner, during the holidays, with Eli reminding her of the wake of destruction she'd never meant to cause. No way, no how—

"I wasn't asking, I was telling." Teddy shook his head. "I'll see you both next Saturday, night before the parade and the Gingerbread Festival."

"Well, then, I'll bring some of my Portuguese sweet bread and some dessert."

"Perfect." Teddy picked up the two tubs of gingerbread. "This is gonna be the best holiday in a long time."

If that was true, then why was her stomach twisting in knots?

THE HEAT WAS cranked up in the teachers' lounge, making Hunter shed his coat and hang it on one of the hooks on the far wall. He made a beeline to the coffeepot. Between Mars's deteriorating condition, the box of baby raccoons left outside the clinic doors and the explosive meltdown of one of his students, he needed a big cup of coffee to keep going. When he got home, he was going to have a couple of glasses of something stronger.

"Thanks for covering at the last minute," he heard Annabeth Upton saying to someone. "When Tyler told me he'd roped you into Career Night, I figured you couldn't say no. Not with your dad's love life in the balance."

He turned to see Annabeth and Jo, chatting just inside the teachers' lounge. He swallowed the last of his coffee and poured himself another. He didn't know how often he'd thought of her, eyes closed and lying in the snow, but the image warmed him from the inside every time.

"They're adorable," Jo said to Annabeth. "If I can just get my dad to man up and court her, I won't have to worry over him being alone."

"Says the woman who insists there's no good in relationships," Annabeth countered.

"I didn't say that." Jo sighed. "I said *I* was no good at relationships."

No good at relationships? His Jo? How could that be? They'd fit together naturally, mind and body. He'd never laughed as much or yelled as loud as he had when he'd been with Jo.

"Because you refuse to try." Annabeth shook her head, seeing him. "Which is a conversation for later. I'm going to make sure everyone's checked in."

Oh, to be a fly on the wall for that conversation. He crumpled the empty coffee cup and threw it in the trash.

"Sure." Jo watched Annabeth walk away before turning to look around the room. She looked a little lost, hesitant. And then she saw him and rolled her eyes. "I should have known you'd be here, Dr. Boone. All impressive in your white coat."

He glanced down at his white coat. "Jealous? I have an extra one in the truck."

She shook her head. "No, no, no. Wouldn't

want anyone to think I could perform an emergency *something* on their…parakeet."

He nodded. "Emergency parakeet procedures are pretty damn tricky."

She laughed, surprising them both. "Good to know."

He tried not to stare at her eyes, her lips, the way she brushed the curls from her shoulder. He cleared his throat. "Here to inspire a future generation of authors?"

"Warn them, really." Jo smiled. "I was a last-minute addition."

"That was real nice of you, Jo." He hoped he wasn't imagining the flush on her cheeks.

"You two ready?" The high school principal, James Klein, asked. "We've got you both in the barn. Sorry, Miss Stephens, George Worley was a farrier, after all. Not the normal setup for an author, I guess. But it's a pretty impressive barn, you'll see."

Hunter tried not to smile at Jo's sigh. She knew all about the high school's barn. It was the place he'd kissed her until they were both dizzy. It had been a very good day. He glanced at her, unable to resist teasing her. "You ever been in the ag barn here, Miss Stephens?"

Her gray eyes went round, then narrowed. "Hmm, I don't think so. Nothing springs to mind."

He pretended to grab his chest. "Ouch."

She nudged him. He nudged her back.

"You started it," she murmured as they entered the barn. "You know that expression—if you can't stand the heat, get out of the kitchen."

"I like the heat, Jo." He winked at her. He missed the heat, her heat. He just didn't know if she'd want to know that. Or if she'd care.

"Dad." Eli sprinted up, his open smile and enthusiasm stamped out as he saw Jo. There was no denying the anger that tightened his jaw. "Miss Stephens," he all but snapped. Hunter didn't know whether his son needed a firm talking to or a long, strong hug.

Hunter watched Jo's startled blink, the effort

it took to make her "Hi, Eli" somewhat cheery. It killed him. To see Eli fuming. To see Jo so hurt. He didn't know how to make it better, for either of them.

"Well—" Jo's voice wavered a bit, making him press his hands against his sides so he wouldn't reach out to her. "I guess I'll go see where I'm supposed to be." She stepped away from them.

"Follow me." Mr. Klein led her to the other side of the barn.

"What's she doing here?" Eli asked, his tone a little too sharp, too hostile.

"She's keeping Tyler Worley from failing algebra, Eli." He looked at the boy. "Watch your tone, son."

Eli frowned at his father, shoving his hands in his pockets.

"Eli." Hunter sighed.

"They set your table up over here." Eli walked away, kicking at bits of straw and dirt as he went.

"Hunter." Mr. Klein hurried up to him. "Would

you mind sharing the space with Miss Stephens? There's a draft over there, something fierce."

"She's got a coat." Eli's grumble was too low for Mr. Klein to hear it, but Hunter did.

"I don't mind at all. Eli, go see if Miss Stephens needs help with anything." The look he gave his son left little room for misinterpretation. This might not be the time to discipline Eli, but the two of them were going to have a serious talk before the night was through. He wasn't about to let his son treat Jo with anything other than respect.

Eli's lips thinned, but he nodded. "Yes, sir."

Five minutes later, he and Jo were introduced to a group of twenty or so kids by the principal. Hunter sat on the edge of the table, letting her go first. It was the polite thing to do and he wanted a few more minutes to just look at her.

"Hi. As Mr. Klein said, I'm Joselyn Stephens. I'm an artist and an author. Art has always been an outlet for me." Jo's voice was soothing. "I used to finger-paint the walls in my parents' house. As you can imagine, that didn't go over well."

He smiled, envisioning a little Jo—all curls and smiles—joyfully smearing colors around the house.

"My parents hid the paint for a few years." The kids laughed. "Once I'd learned that walls weren't the best place to practice, my dad bought me my first art set. He was about to be deployed overseas. He told me to paint him pictures of home. So, instead of letters, I sent him pictures. He was the one who told me my pictures told stories. In time, other stories sort of popped up."

A girls hand shot up and Jo pointed at her.

"Are your stories really about here? Stonewall Crossing?"

Jo shrugged. "Yes." She glanced at Hunter then. "Some of the stories started right here, in this barn." She waved her hand at the empty arenas. "I wasn't very good at the whole animal-raising thing."

"I wouldn't say that." Hunter crossed his arms over his chest, shaking his head.

"Because you're a gentleman." She rolled her eyes and a few kids laughed. So did he. "Anyway, this was so foreign to me. I made notes and did so many sketches on everything that went into raising animals, exercising them, and the importance of stock shows. Once I was done with college, I'd learned how to put together a story. That's when I finished *34*. And, yes, it was based on Dr. Boone's state championship calf. The one that sold for *how* much at auction?"

Hunter waved her question away.

"Were you two *friends*?" a girl asked, the emphasis on *friends* unmistakable.

Hunter glanced out, his gaze wandering over the crowd. But then he saw Eli, standing by the show ring, scowling and frustrated. The way his son looked at Jo broke his heart.

Jo's voice wavered, drawing him back to the conversation. "Yes, we were friends."

"How do you start? Writing, I mean?" Hunter asked her, trying to redirect the conversation.

Jo looked at him, relieved. "The pictures. I have some author friends who don't write picture books and they start with a character. It's a pretty individual process."

"Is college really necessary?" another boy asked.

"I think it is," Jo argued. "I think college is a good move for anyone, no matter what they plan on doing with their life. Think of it as a way to expand your horizons." She paused. "I kind of stepped in here at the last minute. Does anyone have any questions?"

"Is this what you always wanted to do?" a girl asked.

He watched Jo, amazed at the smile that spread across her face. "It is. It makes me happy. I mean, it also makes me really unhappy, like when I get stuck on a story."

Jo stopped then, her smile fading. He followed her gaze to Eli. His son wore a look of pure disdain. Jo's voice distracted him. "But I guess all professions have ups and downs. Right, Dr. Boone?"

"Yes." He swallowed, hoping he didn't look as thrown as he felt. "Definitely."

"How did you get into veterinary medicine?" she asked, sitting on the edge of the table, deferring the floor to him.

"I grew up working with animals. My father and his father and his father before that. I wanted to heal animals early on. Everything from field mice to injured hawks." He pointed at the display board one of his teaching assistants had put together for him. "School was a challenge. I got accepted early, before I had my undergraduate degree. I won't kid you—school is tough and very competitive. But it's important to understand that some things take work to achieve. You have to want it. You have to do the work."

He talked for a while, trying to include Jo in the questions being asked, but she'd withdrawn.

One look at his son spoke volumes. It would be hard to engage when someone was staring daggers at you. And there was no denying the resentment on his son's face.

Chapter Six

"I'm going to walk Lola home," her father announced.

"Now, Carl," Lola argued as she pulled on her thick coat.

He grinned, buttoning Lola's top button. "Hush now. Doc said it would do me some good. Didn't he, Josie?" Her father looked at her.

Josie managed to nod.

"See there?" Carl opened the doors. "Might take me a little longer, though—"

"I don't mind." Lola tucked her hand into his arm, winking at Josie. "Night, sugar."

"Night, Lola." She stared at the empty doorway long after they'd left. Her dad might just be catching a clue. *About time.*

"Jo?" Hunter's voice was soft, his knock on the screen door startling her.

"Hunter?" She braced herself. "Come in."

The past hour had been at once the best and worst time she'd had in a long time. She missed having that spark, that zippy back and forth that she had with Hunter. The way he smiled that crooked smile, arched his brow at her—she didn't know whether she wanted to kiss him or run far, far away.

And then there was Hunter's son. There was also the possibility that Eli's scowl might actually kill her. She'd been on the receiving end of quite a few stare-downs in her time, but she didn't know how to respond to Eli. If only there was something she could do or say to defuse some of his rage.

"Hey," she said, peeking around him, expecting Eli to join them. "How many future vets do you think you made tonight?"

"Maybe a few."

"It's the coat," she teased. "Something about its white splendor is so…so enticing."

"Is it?"

She rolled her eyes. "Why don't you ride on home before you freeze, cowboy?"

He laughed. "I'm going, I'm going, but I keep forgetting to give you this." He pulled a white envelope from his coat pocket. "I know you probably don't have time for this, but I promised I'd pass it along to you."

She stared at the UET Veterinary Medicine envelope. "Is it an order form for my own white coat?"

"You wish."

She chuckled.

Silence set in, long and awkward. She didn't have the nerve to look at him. Not now. Instead, she stared at the envelope in her hands. "Well, thanks for this." She tapped the corner of the envelope in her palm. "It's late—"

"Jo." His voice changed, from teasing to husky and a little too sexy in two minutes flat.

"Oh, am I supposed to open this now?" she asked, tearing the top of the envelope. She pulled out the papers, skimming over the letter. This was a commission? A very well-paid commission. For a mural for the waiting room at the teaching veterinary hospital.

"No." He sighed. "I was…I was wondering if you're free for dinner tomorrow night."

She stared at him, the commission forgotten. "But…" Did he not notice his son's reaction tonight? "Hunter—"

"Jo." His voice was a whisper. He moved forward, his eyes sweeping over her face.

Her entire body seemed to quiver, waiting for his touch. She stepped back but, somehow, he seemed even closer.

"Don't say no." His words were so low, gruff.

She couldn't say anything. Not now, when he was looking at her like that. Instead, she swallowed, searching for some sassy comeback to counter the dangerous warmth spreading through every single cell of her body. In two steps, her back was against the wall.

He stepped forward. "One night. No history. No interruptions. Just me and you."

"A date?" Her question was a whisper.

His hand reached up, gently grasping one of her curls. Something about the way he caressed her hair made her ache for his touch. "What do you say, Jo?" His eyes met hers. Blazing, electric, the pull almost physical. He released the curl, placing his big hands on either side of her head.

She blew out a shaky breath, unable to hide the effect he was having on her. His mouth was so close, his breath caressing her skin. His gaze explored her face, slow and intense. His nostrils flared and his jaw went tight. She sucked in a deep breath and tilted her head, an unmistakable invitation. Her heart kicked into overdrive as he leaned forward. She closed her eyes, waiting, ready, willing, bursting.

His forehead rested against hers.

"I'm not going to kiss you until you say yes," he rasped.

Her eyes popped open. "Yes," she answered quickly, too quickly. Not that there was any point in denying what was happening. They both felt it—they both wanted it.

His gaze searched her face, long and slow. Then he smiled and stepped away from her. He shoved his hands in his pockets and cleared his throat. "I'll pick you up at seven o'clock."

She stared at him, in complete shock. "But… but I didn't—"

"You said yes, Jo," he said softly.

"Hunter, that's not what I was saying yes to."

"What were you saying yes to, then?"

She swallowed. No way she was going to admit she wanted him to kiss her, not with him standing there all cocky. "But my dad—"

"Tomorrow's bingo at the Senior Center. Think they're having a holiday party after that and I'm sure, what with Lola being there and all, he'll be going." He waited.

No arguing now. She stared at him, knowing he'd won. "Okay," she murmured.

"Wear something nice."

"Wear something nice?" she muttered.

His smile grew.

"Why are you smiling like that?" she bit out.

"I feel like smiling." He shrugged.

She tried to glare at him, she really did. But his smile was just too infectious. She liked him smiling. She liked that he could make her want to smile. Like now. In fact, there was no way she could stop the one spreading across her face.

The front door opened. "You two done? I'm getting a touch of frostbite out here." Her father walked in, rubbing his hands together.

"Dad." She wrapped an arm around her dad and led him into the living room. She tugged his recliner closer to the fireplace. "Sit and warm up. I'll make you some hot chocolate."

"Checking on Sprinkles, Hunter?" her dad

asked as he sat. "Come on in and warm up. Josie can make you some hot chocolate, too, can't you, Josie?"

She glanced at Hunter. To her extreme aggravation, he laughed. "I'll have to take you up on that some other night. Eli stayed to help Mrs. Upton clean up, but I imagine he's ready for me to pick him up by now. You still playing bingo at the Senior Center tomorrow night?"

"Wouldn't miss it. Lola's asked a few of us over for a late dinner afterward." She heard the satisfaction in her father's voice.

"So you won't mind if I take Jo out for a bit?" Hunter asked.

She glared at Hunter. Was he asking her father permission? "Oh, please—"

Her father held up his hand. "I'll be honest, Hunter, I have a few concerns. Josie's lighter fluid and you *are* her match. You two left a lot of destruction last time around, for all those that love you."

She paused again, wrapping her arms around

her waist. Her attention fixed on her father. He might be teasing, a little, but he was also making a point. She'd been so angry and hurt, she hadn't stopped to think about anyone but herself, not her father, the Boone family or Hunter. And she sincerely regretted the way she'd shut everyone out. "It was a long time ago, Dad." She tried to sound flippant but failed.

"It was," her father agreed. "But some wounds take a lot of time to heal—if they heal at all."

HUNTER STIFFENED. CARL'S words hung there, too big to ignore. He couldn't help but look at Jo then. The older man was right—some wounds took a long time to heal. He never wanted to open himself up to a hurt like the one he'd felt when Josie had left. It had broken him, clawed at his insides until he'd worried he'd split in two. But she hadn't left because of what had happened with Amy. She'd left him before Amy had been in the picture. She'd left because she'd wanted to.

Her gray eyes were looking everywhere but at him. He wondered about that. Did she know how alone he'd felt? That his love had felt insignificant when she'd tossed it aside so quickly.

Her college admissions letter had been her golden ticket out of Stonewall Crossing. Away from him. He knew the art program in New Mexico was the one she wanted most in the country. And he wanted only the best for her. He'd dropped hints about doing his undergrad work anywhere, but she'd never acknowledged them or asked him to come with her. She'd just left. He didn't blame her for leaving, for following her dreams. But it killed him to know that he hadn't been a part of them. To him, it had been their future. To her, it was about getting out and starting over.

That wound was one he still wasn't over.

What happened after that was all his fault. Jo had been gone for months, her calls getting further and further apart. He'd missed her, missed feeling loved and needed. Amy had been all too willing to ignore his drunken state and lead him home to bed.

Jo had been hurt—he'd hurt her. And he hated himself for what he'd done to her heart. If there was a way to apologize, to undo the heartbreak one tortured night caused so many people, he would. But Eli was the result of that one night, and his son was his life. Even if Jo was still the love of his life.

Hunter realized Jo was watching him, her forehead furrowed. "If you're against it—"

"I didn't say that." Carl waved his hand. "It'll be good for you two to have some time, to work through whatever it is that's there. And enjoy some holiday cheer while you're at it."

Whatever it is that's there. His heart knew exactly what was between them. Jo's gaze met his then and his throat went dry.

"And Sprinkles is fine," Carl went on. "She's been trying to scratch her way through the linoleum for some…" But Hunter was watching the panic creep into Jo's eyes.

She was thinking, overthinking, letting her mind take over and fill in all the silent spaces with doubt. She'd always been real good at letting her head overrule her heart.

"…but she's eating fine," Carl finished.

"Good." Hunter nodded. "Glad to hear it."

Jo was scowling at him. And she looked mighty fine doing it. One look from her made it all too easy to forget any past hurts and move on to their next adventure. He knew the two of them would be better than ever, if she'd give them the chance.

His phone started vibrating. "Eli?" she asked.

He heard the catch in her voice as he checked his phone and glanced her way. "Yep."

She smiled. "It's awful cold, Hunter. Too cold to leave him waiting outside for long."

He shook his head. After the knives his son had been shooting at her all night, he was fine with letting his son suffer a few minutes of cold. "He's fine."

She scowled again. "Hunter—"

"I'm going." He patted Carl on the shoulder. "Enjoy your hot chocolate." He walked right up to Jo. "I'll see you tomorrow night." And, before he could stop himself, he dropped a kiss on her cheek. When he stepped back, her eyes were huge. She might be surprised, but she wasn't angry. If anything, she looked pleased. Not that she was happy about it.

He winked at her, ignoring the way she frowned in irritation, the way she stood straight as if prepping for battle. He touched his hat at Jo, said good-night to Carl and slipped from the house.

It was cold and dark, a steady pelting of icy rain clicking against the sidewalk. But, even with the winter wind cutting through his thick Carhartt jacket, he wasn't too bothered. If anything, he was excited. It had been a long time since anticipation warmed him.

"Took you long enough," Eli mumbled when Hunter arrived at the high school. But he didn't let his son's tone or long-suffering sighs get to him. Instead, he turned up the radio, blasting Christmas carols the entire ride home.

Once he'd closed the door behind him, he turned to find Eli waiting. "Dad," his son began.

He put his hands on his hips. Eli had no idea how close he'd come to being publically put in his place. "Yep?"

"I owe you an apology."

That was the last thing he expected to hear. "You do?"

"Yes, sir." Eli looked at him. "I was disrespectful."

"To me?" he asked, trying not to feel impatient.

Eli's mouth pressed shut.

Hunter sighed. "Why do you think you owe me an apology? You weren't bound and determined to make me uncomfortable tonight."

"I wasn't trying to make anyone uncomfortable tonight."

Hunter shook his head and hung up his hat and coat. "Now you should apologize."

"I just did," Eli shot back.

"No—" Hunter folded his arms across his chest. "Not for your behavior tonight. But for the lie you just told."

Hunter watched his son. Eli had a temper on him, but he'd never let it slip. It killed Hunter to see his son's hands fist, see the raw anger twisting his boy's features. That was bad. But watching his son turn, storm out of the room and slam his bedroom door shut behind him made Hunter feel as if he'd been kicked in the gut.

Chapter Seven

Josie was tired, bone-tired. But watching Dara and Lola at work, being part of their comfortable chatter, made the daylong baking less of a chore. When Dara and her father had shown up early this morning looking for breakfast, Josie had offered to let Dara stay and bake while he did some holiday shopping. Lola had knocked on the door at seven, bringing in a basket of fresh biscuits and some fresh jam, and set to work alongside them. They'd been mixing, baking and decorating gingerbread, sharing stories and laughing the whole time. At the rate they were going, they just might have a complimentary cookie for everyone in Stonewall Crossing.

Dara piped an icing smile onto the ginger-bread girl she was finishing, then placed a small gummy spice drop right in the middle of the bow she'd made. Josie watched the girl, noting the satisfaction on her young face. "Sure you've never done this before?" she asked.

Dara shook her head. "My mom doesn't like to bake. If she can't buy it at the store, we don't have it at our place."

Lola clicked her tongue. "Well, that's just wrong. Baking is good for the soul." She paused, winking at them both. "If not for the waistline."

They laughed.

"You're welcome to lend a hand anytime," Josie added. "Once you're old enough to hire, believe me, I'll tell Dad to hire you."

"He does too much on his own. The ol' coot," Lola agreed. "Would do him some good to hire some help."

Josie agreed. When she couldn't sleep, she'd

organized her father's financials. He was making a tidy profit. He didn't need to be a one-man show. Josie loved seeing him relaxing, putting on a little weight, smiling and laughing. He needed to get out, to have a life beyond the four walls of his bakery. With Lola Worley.

"If I can convince my mom." Dara sounded a little wistful.

"She doesn't want you working?" Lola asked. Lola, Josie noted, didn't mince words when it came to conversations. "A woman should have skills."

Josie agreed. But there were women, her mother included, who still believed the best career a woman could have was marrying a rich man. Her mother's idea of a well-rounded education had included pouting, exercising and the importance of thorough grooming. Aging gracefully was a concept her mother disdained. She claimed it was an excuse for letting yourself go and getting complacent.

"I think my mom worries about me. She doesn't want me to be a housewife. She wants me to be a lawyer or doctor or something." Dara shrugged, her cheeks turning a deep red. "I like making things."

"What do you want to do?" Josie asked the girl.

"I don't really know. Do I have to? Right now?" The young girl looked between them both.

"No." Lola laughed.

"Sometimes I still don't know," Josie added.

Annabeth arrived. "Hey, guys. Sorry, Cody's playdate got started late. What did I miss?"

"Dara wants to know when she has to decide what she wants to be," Josie said.

Annabeth frowned. "Ugh. Not for years and years?"

"Good." Dara sighed. "I'm more interested in learning to drive and what my first kiss will be like."

Josie, Annabeth and Lola shared a smile.

"Sounds about right to me." Lola gave Dara a one-armed hug.

"You remember your first kiss?" Dara asked Lola.

"Of course I do." Lola nodded, moving cookies from the baking pan to the cooling rack. "It was with Theodore Boone."

"Really?" Josie glanced at the woman.

"Do tell," Annabeth said as she washed her hands before jumping into the cookie making.

Lola nodded, a look of pride on her face. "I was a looker and the menfolk were all very flattering. Of course, Magnolia hadn't moved to town yet, so I didn't have much competition. But he was sweet on me. So was my Henry. In the end, Henry was the right pick—even if Teddy was a better kisser." She giggled. "Henry got better, in time. You have to train them right."

Josie laughed, taking note of Dara's round eyes and startled expression.

"Speaking of first kisses, I'm assuming Hunter was yours?" Lola asked Josie.

Josie nodded, staring at the dough.

"Take after his daddy?" Lola asked. "Meaning, he knows how to kiss a girl?"

Dara made a strange little noise at the back of her throat.

Annabeth giggled and Josie sighed. "Lola—"

Lola looked back and forth between the younger women. "What?" She waved a dismissive hand at Josie. "Dara should know what she's got to look forward to. It's plain to see Eli's sweet on her."

Dara squeaked this time.

"Lola." Josie couldn't help but laugh then.

"Fine, fine." The older woman went back to rolling out a new batch of dough, grinning from ear to ear.

After a few minutes of companionable silence, Dara asked, "Where's Dr. Boone taking you tonight, Miss Stephens? Not much to do around here, unless you're playing bingo."

Lola nodded. "And no offense to you, sweetie,

but you two are too young to be hanging out with my crowd tonight."

"What?" Annabeth tossed some flour at Josie. "You're going on a date?"

"Yes." Josie smiled. "I don't know where we're going or what we're doing. He just said to wear something nice."

Lola looked thoughtful. Dara and Annabeth looked excited. So why did she feel petrified?

"Nice?" Lola tapped her chin with one finger. "Hmm, sounds like he's got *something* planned."

Josie nodded. That was why she'd spent most of the night tossing and turning, wondering what Hunter had planned—what he was thinking. No answers were coming, so she'd climbed out of bed and started baking. At 3:00 a.m. She stared down at her flour-covered shirt. "I'll definitely need a shower."

Dara giggled. "Don't worry, Miss Stephens. You're one of the prettiest women I've ever met."

"Isn't she?" Annabeth smiled.

"And just as nice on the inside, too," Lola

agreed. "Where it matters most." Lola looked at the young girl. "Don't you let anyone tell you different, either, Dara, you hear?"

"Yes, ma'am."

Josie nodded in silent agreement with Lola. If her father was man enough to make an honest woman out of Lola Worley, she'd finally have the mother she always wanted. Lots of advice, love and willingness to lend a hand when needed. Nothing like her flesh-and-blood, look-but-don't-touch mother.

"I wouldn't worry too much about what you wear," Lola said. "It's clear that boy's got it bad for you."

Lola's words were hardly comforting. It's not that she didn't want Hunter to have feelings for her… Wait, she didn't want that. Did she?

Dara stopped piping icing onto the cookie and said, "That's true, Miss Worley. The way he looks at you, Miss Stephens." She sighed. "Like a present on Christmas morning. It's like he wants to talk to you, you know? Really talk to you. Like he has something important to say, but he's too nervous."

Josie stared at the girl, torn. Did Hunter really look at her like that?

"He's always looked at her like that." Annabeth laughed. "He looks like that when he talks about her."

Lola arranged a fresh tray of cookies on the cooling rack. "It's the way a man should look at the woman he loves—"

"Lola," Josie cut her off. "I think… I think I'll wear a dress. Maybe?"

"He's not the only nervous one." Lola nudged Dara.

Dara glanced at Josie. "Is that normal? To feel all…" The girl shrugged. "Out of sorts, in a good way, of course. Like you can't stop thinking about them. Even when you want to stomp on their foot and never talk to them again?" Dara added with a hint of agitation.

It took a lot to keep Josie from laughing.

"Oh, most definitely," Lola agreed. "The more irate they make you, the fiercer the love is."

"Within reason, Dara," Josie offered. "Fireworks are fun, but they can be destructive."

The others looked at her again, this time without the smiles.

"How are things going with my father?" Josie asked, needing a diversion. And because she was curious.

"You and Mr. Stephens?" Dara looked shocked.

"It can happen," Lola said. "Even at my age."

Dara shook her head. "I didn't mean that, Miss Worley. I guess I didn't think Mr. Stephens was all that aware of women."

"Oh, honey, men are always aware of women." Lola started cutting out new cookies to put on the tray. "Some of them are too old to do anything about it."

Josie sincerely hoped her father did not fall into that category.

"And some men have been too burned to know

how to try again." Lola was looking at her as she said that last part.

"Maybe they shouldn't. Maybe they should move on," she murmured.

"Man's heart doesn't always wander the way his eye does, Joselyn. I'd hazard to say quite a few fellas I know are far more true-blue than a lot of lady friends I have." Lola put a new tray of cookies into the oven.

"Listen to your heart," Annabeth added.

"Isn't that a song?" Josie tried to tease.

"Oh, stop it. I'm serious. Do what you can to make your heart and soul happy." Annabeth spoke with such force Josie paused. Yes, Dara was young and naive and full of hope. But Annabeth and Lola had been married, happily. Maybe she shouldn't dismiss what they had to say.

What did she want? What did she really want?

They spent the next few hours listening to music, sharing stories and laughing. They taught Dara to do the chicken dance. Lola taught them the twist. And Josie's dad joined them long enough to share chicken and dumplings for lunch.

"I'd best be heading home," Lola said, hanging her apron on the hook by the counter. "Not much time to pull myself together before the festivities tonight."

"Thank you for all your help," Josie said as she hugged the woman.

"No problem at all." Lola smiled. "You have fun tonight," she said, pulling the door shut behind her.

"I should probably head out, too." Dara hung her apron beside Lola's. She glanced at Josie. "The thing is, I really like Eli. Or I did. But now that he's acting rude, I'm not so sure."

Annabeth looked at the young girl. "Eli's been rude to you, too? I couldn't believe the way he acted at Career Night."

"Oh, no, not me." She blushed, shaking her head. "But toward you, Miss Stephens—"

Josie shrugged. There was no denying the way Eli felt about her.

"I know he's worried his dad's going to get his heart broken. Oops, sorry." She looked at Josie. "I think it's sweet that he wants to protect his dad, but not how he's going about it. I mean, can't he just talk to his dad? Can't they come to some sort of understanding?"

"Men don't talk the way women do." Annabeth sighed. "They'll work it out, eventually."

Josie felt sick to her stomach. What was she thinking? Why was she considering going out with Hunter, knowing that his son was dead set against her. She tried to smile at Dara. "Try not to be too hard on him, Dara. I know he's a good kid."

"It's natural for him to be worried. Maybe even a little jealous, too, since Hunter hasn't been interested in another woman…well, ever." Annabeth laughed. "You're uncharted territory."

Josie nodded. "I need to talk to Eli. I would never come between him and his dad. He's been lucky to have a strong family all his life. I don't want him to think I'd try to change that."

Dara's father showed up shortly afterward. Josie and Annabeth sent them on their way with a plate of Dara's cookies.

"You ready for tonight?" Annabeth asked. "Do we need to have *the* talk?"

Josie rolled her eyes. "Um, I don't think so."

"Just don't get too far into your head, Josie. Try to have fun. Try to remember that this is the guy you loved with your whole heart." She hugged Josie. "And try to remember that if you marry him you'll live here and we can hang out and have fun."

The bakery was too quiet once Annabeth left. All Josie's fears and insecurities reared up, reminding her how clearly wrong tonight was. She should get out of town earlier, put a few thousand miles between Hunter and her heart, for all their sakes. It was the right thing to do. Her dad was getting better now that he was listening to the doctor. And Lola was around to help keep him on the road to recovery. Now she needed a way out of tonight.

The phone rang. "Pop's Bakery," she answered.

"Wear your sexy underwear." Annabeth's voice was laced with laughter. "Not your cotton granny panties."

Josie groaned. "There will be no underwear viewing tonight." She chewed on her lip. "As a matter of fact, my head is killing me—"

"No, it's not," Annabeth argued.

"Yes, it—"

"Stop it, Josie," Annabeth snapped. "You're fine."

"It's my head. I think I know when I'm getting a headache."

"Oh, please. You are chicken."

Josie sighed. "Maybe. A little."

"Well, that's just pathetic. I have to get my kicks from naughty texts, while you're passing up on the real deal."

Josie's interest was piqued. "Naughty texts? With who?"

"No one you'd know," Annabeth huffed in exasperation. "Besides, texts can't compare to actual kissing and touching. Period."

There was a pause.

"Does your head really hurt?" Annabeth asked.

Josie closed her eyes. "A little."

"Fine. Take Advil. Cancel tonight and add it to your list of regrets. Go to bed. Whatever."

"Gosh, thanks."

"You can't expect me to support your life on the sidelines, Josie, you just can't. Your *dad* is getting more action than you are."

"Um, gross." Josie winced. "I'll call you tomorrow."

"Sure, I guess," Annabeth muttered. "I mean, if there's anything to tell."

She hung up, put the cookies away and did a lightning-fast cleanup of the kitchen. She stopped to nudge her father awake before heading to the shower. A long, steamy, hot shower gave her time to consider her options. Lola and Annabeth said to listen to her heart, but Annabeth also said to listen to her libido. Unfortunately, or fortunately depending on how you looked at it, both her heart and her libido were supremely interested in spending the evening with Hunter Boone.

She could cancel tonight, book a flight and leave first thing in the morning. But then she'd be letting people down…again. And, dammit, she didn't want to be that sort of person. She didn't want to be her mother.

Okay, fine, then she was staying. She was going on the date with Hunter. And she was not going to overanalyze everything that happened.

Her closet didn't have much to offer. She'd packed for caregiving and nights in with her dad, not dates or a night on the town. She had one black dress, no frills. A clingy wrap dress that was cut low but traveled well. Her only real option.

She laid the dress out on the bed and opened her underwear drawer. Pretty silky garments or practical cotton foundation wear. That was the real question.

Chapter Eight

Hunter tugged at the collar of his shirt, adjusting the collar and tie for the fifth time since he'd parked in front of Pop's Bakery. He felt like an idiot. He was too old to be getting dressed up, to feel this tongue-tied and flustered.

Eli was right. What was he thinking? A vision of his fuming, red-faced son didn't ease the knot in his throat or the twist in his gut. They'd never argued like that, ever. The two of them were thick as thieves, working through any disagreement without losing their cool. He'd raised his son to be rational, looking at a situation from all sides, putting himself in the other person's shoes and keeping an open mind. And, thank God, Eli was like him—no drama.

But when it came to Jo, Amy had planted a seed of hate deep in his son. He hadn't realized just how deep until Jo got here, until he saw the look in his son's eyes and knew how much he blamed Jo for his and Amy's divorce.

Was he a bad father for leaving Eli angry and taking Jo on a date? Was he selfish for wanting time with her? Eli sure as hell thought so. Tonight was something Hunter had to do. If he didn't try, if he let Jo slip away, the regret would cripple him.

He pushed the truck door open, a blast of frosty wind forcing it wide. Pulling his jacket tight around him, he hurried up onto the porch, out of the wind. But then he froze, staring at the door, nervous and uncertain all over again.

He was about to knock when he heard a strange thumping followed by a highly frustrated shriek.

"Sprinkles!" He knew that sound. Jo was fit to be tied. And Hunter couldn't stop the smile that spread across his face. "Stop, dammit, I need that."

Clicking, probably Sprinkles nails on the wood floor, followed by more thumps. He knocked, but there was no answer. He waited, then eased the door open. "Hello?"

"Come on, Sprinkles, give it to me." Jo's voice was muffled. "If you're a good girl, I'll give you a treat." Sprinkles barked in answer.

He closed the door, sealing the cold out. "Jo?"

"I swear, dog." Each word was getting louder, less coaxing. "I will buy more face cream and leave it out just for you."

He chuckled, following the sound of her voice into the back of the house. "Jo?"

"That's it, Sprinkles," she cooed. "Just a little closer."

He found her then. Halfway under her bed, her fuzzy robe revealing two long, toned legs and barely covering her mighty fine rump. "Jo?" He cleared his throat.

Jo squeaked, rearing up. A distinct thud made him wince. "Damn, Jo, you okay?"

Her groan was muffled. "I see stars." She pushed herself out from under the bed, one hand coming up to hold her head.

He knelt beside her. "I didn't mean to scare you. I knocked, I promise."

"Yeah, well, I didn't hear you."

He nodded.

Her face was screwed up tight from pain. "I'm not exactly ready."

"I got that."

She opened her eyes, scowling at him. "Damn dog ran off with my stockings. Once she'd decided she was done with them, she took off with my brush."

"How'd the stockings hold up?" he asked.

She shook her head. "They'll be good for tying up Dad's tomato plants in the spring." She rubbed her temple. "Ouch. Goose egg."

He leaned forward, noting the red welt rising along her hairline. "You always did have a knack for scrapes." He tilted her head back, trying not to appreciate her bared creamy shoulder or the long curve of her graceful neck. "Let's get some ice on that."

She sighed, pointing under the bed. "*She* still has my brush. And unless this—" she pointed at herself "—is acceptable for a night out, I need it."

"Let's get some ice." He stood and held out his hand to her. "Then we'll get the brush." He pulled her up, catching a whiff of citrus and soap. She smelled like heaven.

"I meant to be ready. I did." She reached up to cradle her head. "That dog hates me."

Hunter chuckled. "She's probably a little jealous of you."

Jo paused, disbelief plain on her face. "Jealous?"

"Sure. You're an interloper." He led her into the kitchen, putting ice into a clean kitchen towel. "It's natural for her to assert her dominance. Or try."

"I thought that meant peeing on my shoe or something." Jo took the ice pack and pressed it to her head. "Thank you for the ice."

"I didn't mean to scare you, Jo."

She smiled, waving his apology away. "I know." Her expression changed, nerves and uncertainty clouding her clear gray eyes. She fidgeted, tugging her robe down while trying to smooth her hair. Her hand landed on one of the large rollers covering her head and her eyes went round. She froze, shook her head and sighed, closing her eyes. "My mother would die. No, no, she would disown me for this." She pressed the ice to her forehead.

He laughed. "I won't tell." He paused. "But I'll see if I can get your brush for you. I don't know if the museum has a dress code or not, but I'm pretty sure hair rollers and bathrobes aren't on the short list."

She adjusted her ice pack so she could level him with a sexy-as-hell, narrow-eyed smile. "Museum?" She was interested, he could tell.

"An Impressionist exhibition. A few Monets. Still your favorite?" Her anger gave way to surprise, then pleasure…then something else that was warm and promising. His lungs emptied, hard and fast.

He stooped, breaking the connection to search cabinets. He didn't want to get sidetracked from the night he'd planned. If he wasn't careful, it'd be all too easy to get lost in her silver-gray eyes. He kept searching until he found the dog treats. "Good thing there's a lock on this one." He pulled the bag from the cabinet and shook it. Jo, he noticed, was pulling rollers from her hair and tucking them into her robe pockets. She was awkward and nervous and all sweet, soft woman.

"Does my head look bad?" she asked, smoothing her hair before holding the ice back to her temple.

He shook his head but didn't trust himself to speak. Instead, he called, "Sprinkles. Come on, girl." He kept shaking the bag, hoping the crackle it made would be too hard for the little dog to resist. It was. The rapid *tap tap* of Sprinkles's claws announced her speedy arrival. She sat, putting her little paws up to beg. He gave Sprinkles a biscuit and graced Jo with a smug smile.

"Oh, please." Jo sighed. "Really?"

"I get this from all the girls," he teased.

Jo burst out laughing then. "I bet you do." She stood, setting the ice and towel in the sink. "I'll leave the two of you alone while I go recover my brush…and anything else she's hidden under the bed."

He watched her go. Her pockets might be bulging with rollers, but the sway of her hips was unmistakable.

Sprinkles scratched his jeans.

"That's how it is?" he asked, giving the dog another biscuit. "You don't deserve another one, picking on Jo like that."

Sprinkles whimpered, spinning around twice.

"Yeah, you're cute and you know it."

Sprinkles sat and yapped at him, ears perked forward.

"No!" Jo's cry had Hunter headed back down the hall to her room.

"What now?" he asked, leaning against her door frame.

She spun, holding her dress out to him. "Hates me." Holding up the dress, it was clear to see a series of tiny teeth marks along the little slit up the back of the dress.

"I can stitch it," he offered. "Believe me, this is nothing." He took the dress from her, inspecting the tear. "Needle and thread?" He glanced at Jo to find her staring at him, her expression thoughtful.

"Hunter, I can wear something else." She glanced around her room.

He did, too. "Uh-huh." Organization wasn't one of Jo's strong suits.

She grinned at him. "Fine." She hurried out of the bedroom, returning minutes later with what looked like a mini black suitcase. She handed it to him. "Thank you. Again."

"My pleasure." He took the dress and bag and headed back into the living room. "I'll let you finish your hair or whatever." Because if he stayed there, in her disaster of a bedroom, he'd never want to leave.

JOSIE SUCKED IN a deep breath as she climbed into the truck. "I'm sorry about tonight."

"What for?"

"Where should I start? Finding me crawling around on the floor in a robe. Having to apply first aid on my head, sewing my dress up—"

He laughed, a deep, rich sound that filled the cab. "That's not exactly the way it happened."

"Storyteller, remember?" she teased.

"Not the way your dates normally start?" he asked, still smiling. He started the truck and backed up, pulling down Main Street.

"If I had a normal dating protocol, I'd have to

say no." She laughed then. "What about you? I guess playing doctor is a possibility—"

"Nope." He shrugged. "Not much opportunity, between work and Eli and all."

"No?" She didn't want to point out that she'd been here for less than two weeks and he'd found the time to cook her dinner, make a house call for her dad and take her on a date. "I can't imagine how hard it is, being a single parent." Not that she hadn't thought about being a mom. She had, a lot. But motherhood meant relationships and that, she knew, wasn't going to happen.

He shook his head. "Not really, not for me, anyway. It's more like Eli's got four fathers. And my dad and sister, Renata, make sure to spoil him now and then."

Eli was lucky to have so much love. Eli, who couldn't be happy about his father's date tonight. She sighed, not wanting to think about the rage she'd seen in the young boy's eyes, not tonight. "So, what do you do, besides work and fatherhood?"

"That's about it, Jo," he answered, amused. "A man's gotta sleep."

She sighed. "So you're a hobbyless, dateless hermit?"

He chuckled. "What about you?"

"I work, a lot. And when I'm not doing murals or teaching classes or working on a book, I'm painting. You know me..." She broke off, glancing at him. "Guess I haven't changed all that much."

He looked at her. "Not much." He turned his attention back to the road, but she saw the way his hands tightened on the steering wheel and wondered at it. "Dad mentioned a new job. Does that mean you're moving?"

She nodded. "New Mexico Art Institute offered me an artist-in-residency position. It could be a great opportunity. Guess it's time for me to think about putting down some roots."

"And New Mexico is where you want to be?" If it was, that was all the answer he needed.

"I don't know. After spending the day with

Annabeth, Lola and Dara, I've learned one thing. I'm not sure what I want. Except that, if I don't make some decisions, I'll be homeless and unemployed." Her laugh sounded forced— she heard it. But she was beginning to wonder if the job, the move, the starting over, was really what she wanted.

"That's not true, Jo. You'll always have a home. Carl would love to have you back in Stonewall Crossing. I know it's not where you imagined yourself ending up, but—"

"I don't mind it," she admitted. When she'd been lying there, wide-awake, she'd mulled over the possibility of staying there longer. Her new story idea was really shaping up. Who knew, if she stayed, maybe more ideas would come. "Stonewall Crossing, I mean."

"No?" He sounded surprised.

"Not anymore. Time and distance can put things into serious perspective. I was so…so ready to escape. Not that I had anything to escape from, but I didn't get that then. Dad was good to me, more than good. Things were stable." She dared to glance at him. "I...I was young. And stupid. And scared."

"Of?"

"Life has shown me one thing, Hunter. When things *were* good, when I was safe or happy, it wasn't going to last. If I stayed and..." She didn't finish the sentence, because she'd lost Hunter, anyway. She'd left because she was too scared to fight for him, to trust him, and her worst fears were realized. "Like I said, I was young and stupid. Somehow I thought leaving would make it less painful—since it was my choice."

"Jo." He sighed. "Your mom's version of family and love was messed up. I won't argue with that. But you had Carl. You had people who wanted you to stay." His tone was hard. "People who would have gone with you, if you'd asked."

People who would have gone with you, if you'd asked. She stared at him, stunned. Was he talking about him? Was he—

His phone started ringing. He pressed a button on the steering wheel. "Dr. Boone."

"Hunter, Archer here." The clipped voice spilled into the truck cab. "Mars is in trouble."

Hunter's head dipped, his voice tight. "Define *trouble.*"

"Accelerated heart rate. Labored breathing. Hold on." There was some background noise, rustling and voices. "Pups are fine at the moment. You'd wanted me to let you know if something changed, so I am."

Even in the dim illumination, she could see Hunter's jaw lock.

"You need to go?" she asked. She didn't know who Mars was, but Hunter was worried. If Hunter needed to be with Mars, then that's where they needed to be. "Let's go."

"There's no reason for you to come in," Archer said. "I can handle this."

"Hi, Archer," Josie called. "I was just telling Hunter I wanted to come visit the hospital, you know, without Sprinkles as a patient."

"You sure?" Hunter asked, already pulling onto the shoulder of the road.

She nodded. "Absolutely."

His crooked smile warmed her heart. "All right. I'll be there in twenty minutes." And he hung up, pulling across the empty four-lane road and heading back to town. "Are you sure you don't want me to take you home?"

"Sounds like you need to get there. And I'd be up for a tour of the hospital, after you save the day in your dashing white coat, of course."

"You said it was irresistible," he reminded her, grinning broadly.

"Did I?"

He sighed, shaking his head.

"I know you can't talk about the case. Doctor-patient confidentiality and all that," she teased. "But I *am* curious."

He shook his head. "Why doesn't that surprise me?"

"Do you always get attached to your patients?"

"No." He smiled. "But every once in a while,

an animal stands out. Depends on their personality, their nature. Just like people."

"That makes sense," she agreed. "Some people are way more likable than others."

He laughed. "Ain't that the truth?"

"You just said *ain't*." She giggled.

He shot her a look as he turned into the parking lot and parked in front of the large glass doors. The lights cut through the dark, casting a welcoming glow into the cold night. "Mars is a sweet thing." He got out of the truck.

Before he could come around and open the door, she hopped out. "You don't have time to be all gentlemanly right now." She hooked her arm through his and pulled him toward the door.

The thick glass doors slid open without a sound and four faces peered at them over the admissions desk.

"Dr. Boone," one of the young men said. "Dr. Boone…er, your brother is in OR 1 waiting for you."

"Dr. Boone, don your super coat and save

Mars." She glanced at him. "Okay, admit it, that sounded *hilarious*."

He laughed, reaching up one hand to stroke her cheek. She froze, her heart racing and her lungs desperately seeking air while his intense blue-green eyes bore into hers.

"Good luck," she whispered.

He nodded. "Be back soon." His attention wandered to the fourth-year students at the desk and his hand fell to his side. He shot her a small smile, then disappeared behind the swinging door labeled Staff Only.

She waved at the students sitting behind the admissions desk before taking in the waiting room of the teaching hospital. Last time she was here, she'd been too caught up in her father and Sprinkles to appreciate the facility. She read over one of the framed articles hanging on the wall, baffled by the list of contributors and clinicians praising the work done at the school and the educators on staff. UET wasn't just one of the best teaching hospitals in the country but, apparently, the world. *Good for you, Hunter.* The sting of tears surprised her, but the swell of pride didn't. She'd always known Hunter was capable of anything.

Movement distracted her, drawing her attention to the massive aquarium full of brilliantly colored fish and coral. She wandered closer, watching the rich sunshine-yellow, vibrant cobalt-blue and fiery-red fish hide behind whatever cover they had.

"Would you like some coffee?" a young woman asked.

Josie turned around. "No, thank you." Her stomach grumbled, loudly. "But I'm starving. Have you guys eaten? And where can a girl order pizza around here?"

Chapter Nine

Hunter stroked Mars's head. "You did good." He spoke softly, noting the dog's respirations and heart rate on her chart. Normal. They'd made the decision to go ahead with the surgery on her back tonight, since the dog would already be sedated. A few pins in three vertebrae. They'd realigned her spine and alleviated the stress off her compressed nerves. In a few days, they should know if Mars would recover use of her legs.

"She'll be fine." Archer checked Mars's IV solution. "Puppies are, too. I told you there was nothing to worry about."

Hunter glanced at his brother. Archer wasn't a fan of small-animal medicine. His passion was large animals, not someone's lapdog. If Mars had been a bull or even a mountain lion, Archer would be over-the-top excited right now. Instead, his brother was almost bored.

"Cute puppies," one of the students, Lori or Linda or something, said.

Hunter nodded. They were. Two yellow and one feisty chocolate. All healthy and, undoubtedly, hungry. "Need to get some formula mixed up." He washed his hands, mentally going over Mars's chart again.

"I can do that, Dr. Boone," Marco, one of the veterinary assistants, offered. "Tonight was awesome, totally awesome, getting to assist."

"Nothing too edge of your seat." Archer led him to the door. "Go on, Hunter, finish your date."

Hunter clapped his brother on the shoulder. "Thanks for the call and the help."

"I would say that's what brothers are for, but this is also my job." Archer tucked his glasses into his coat pocket and headed toward his office.

Hunter laughed, making his way from the operating room and through the maze of hallways and patient rooms to the front desk. When he pushed through the waiting room doors, he found Jo standing on top of a chair, measuring the wall with a yardstick. Two of his students stood nearby, watching Jo as she teetered on one foot.

"Do I want to know?" he asked, crossing to Jo. She'd twisted her hair up, two pencils sticking out of the messy bun at the nape of her neck.

"Hey." She was all smiles, for him. And he liked it. "How did it go? Is Mars okay?"

"Fine." He nodded.

"Puppies, too?"

"Puppies, too." He wanted to grab her out of that chair and hold her close. "What are you up to?"

She frowned at him. "I'm not up to anything."

"You're standing on a chair with a yardstick." He arched an eyebrow and waited.

"I had to do something while you were working."

"And that would be?" he asked, aware that both students were trying to edge their way back to the admissions desk without being noticed.

"Nothing." She held her hand out to him, rolling her eyes in exasperation. He took her hand, noticing for the first time that she was barefoot. He helped her step down from the chair, smiling down at her.

"What?" she asked.

"You're just so damn cute."

She grinned. "You're not so bad yourself, Dr. Boone." She smoothed her hands over his shoulders, her fingers skimming the collar of his white lab coat. "It's the coat."

He had trouble focusing. "Hungry?"

She shook her head. "We got pizza." She pulled him over to the admissions desk. Five boxes of pizza were spread over the counter. "They were hungry. I figured you'd be hungry, so—"

"You bought pizza." He looked at the students. "Been a quiet night?" he asked them. "No calls?"

One of the students jumped up, reading from the call log. "We did have one call about a dog that couldn't go to the bathroom."

Hunter shook his head. "Talk about an eventful night."

"So, pizza?" Jo asked. "Canadian bacon and mushroom?" Which was his all-time favorite pizza. She'd remembered.

He nodded, taking the box one of the students offered, watching Jo cross the waiting room to a set of chairs. That's when he saw the papers spread across them.

It was the mural, the note from Dr. Lee and several more pages stapled together. "The commission?"

She nodded, holding up the picture, then looking at the wall.

He sat, holding the pizza box in his lap. "You

200 A Cowboy's Christmas Reunion

thinking about it?" He pulled a slice of pizza out, waiting, nervous.

She glanced at him, the picture, the wall, then him again. "You said it—the only guarantee in my future is uncertainty. I guess…" She swallowed, looking at the picture in her hands. "I guess I'm toying with the idea of staying. For a while, maybe."

"Good plan," he managed, taking a huge bite of pizza before his smile revealed how happy she'd just made him.

She turned to him. "It's a lovely idea. The mural, I mean."

He nodded. "You ready for that tour?" he asked, grabbing another slice and standing. "Might help you make up your mind about the mural." And staying.

She tucked all the papers back into an envelope. "Lead on doctor."

And he did. They toured the exam rooms, the pre-op area, the post-op area, the operating rooms, the lecture halls—pretty much anything that would impress her, he showed her. The hospital was just as big a part of his life as the ranch, and her opinion mattered. And then he pulled out the big guns.

"These are Mars's puppies." He pointed to the three pups wiggling around on a heat pad wrapped in soft blankets.

"Poor little things." Jo's forehead creased. "Think they're looking for their mom?"

He smiled. "That blanket belongs to Mars. They're getting plenty of mama-scent and not having to fight to eat. Bottle-fed pups have it easy."

"Where's mom?"

"She'll be sleeping for a while. If she's all right, we'll put them with her for a while tomorrow. We'll just wait and see." He reached into the box, cradling one of the pups in his hand. "She'll do better with her babies around her." He assessed the puppy, turning it over, lifting its head, running his fingers over the small stomach and smiling when it whimpered.

"Pass inspection?" Jo asked, watching him. Her eyes seemed to make note of everything he did without revealing a thing.

He set the puppy back on the mat. "This wasn't what I had planned for tonight."

"So I shouldn't be flattered you arranged all this—" she pointed at the puppies "—for me."

He stepped closer. "Is that what you're feeling? Flattered?" Her cheeks turned a rosy red and hope bloomed in his chest. He reached up, pulling the pencils from her hair. It tumbled around her shoulders.

She held his gaze, her voice husky. "What are you up to, Dr. Boone?"

"Kissing you," he answered, cupping her face in his hands.

Her breath hitched before she stepped in toward him, tilting her head back.

He bent his head, his mouth finding hers, sealing them together. He groaned and pulled her against him. Her curves made thought impossible, but he could hear alarm bells ringing in his head. He softened his kiss, keeping it tender, gentle and teasing.

Before he lost himself to the feel of her, he stepped back and drew air deep into his lungs. "It's late," he whispered. But the sight of her made the fire in his stomach burn higher. Her eyes were still closed, her face still angled for his kiss. "Jo?"

Her eyes opened, heavy-lidded and dazed.

He pulled her back against him. One hungry look was all it would take to make him forget about going slow. His arm kept her close while his fingers traced the side of her face. "I should get you home." He needed to say it, out loud, so he'd do it.

She blinked in confusion. Her cheeks flushed a deep red as she put some space between the two of them. She took his hand in hers and nodded.

"THANKS FOR THE RIDE," Dara said, climbing out of Josie's little red rental car.

"Thank you for all your hard work." Jo put the

car in Park. "Dad's cookies always taste good, but I don't think they've ever looked so pretty. I know people will be really impressed at the parade, Dara."

The girl's blush was precious.

"Do you need help carrying any of this?" Josie glanced in the backseat at the bags of lights Dara had brought to decorate the float.

"I can make a couple of trips if you need to get back," Dara said.

"The bakery's closed. Between Dad and Lola, I think they've got things under control." She smiled at the girl and turned the car off. "I didn't want to be the third wheel." She was very pleased to see her father kiss Lola on the cheek this morning, in front of half of Stonewall Crossing. She figured the other half knew all about it by now. "Besides, the weather's too pretty to miss." For the first time in three days, the sun was warm and the breeze wasn't frigid. She climbed out of the car and popped the trunk, revealing more lights and some green plastic garland.

If she was completely honest with herself, she wanted to stay. This was where her story was coming from. The parade, the holiday, the float. Something about those lights in the park, all warm and brilliant, like the colors of Christmas wrap and holiday dresses, had started her off. Then the float, the kids, all stacking up to be a wonderful holiday story of small-town Texas life—what she wrote and illustrated best.

The fact that they were putting together the float at Boone Ranch was another perk.

She'd fallen asleep with the searing memory of Hunter's kiss still hot on her lips. It wasn't as if she hadn't been kissed plenty of times—she had. But this was more than a kiss. And, since she was admitting things to herself, she might as well face the fact that she was falling in love all over again. She just didn't know what to do about it.

"Hey, Josie." Fisher joined them. "Looks like you got here just in time."

"Oh?" she asked, looking up at him.

"We were about to head into town, for more of these." He reached into the trunk and pulled out the garland. "Eli, Tyler, Rogan!" he called, waving them over to her car. "You staying to help?"

"If you need it," she said, risking a glance at the boys hurrying to the trunk.

"More help is always needed," Fisher said. "Come on."

"Man, Dara, you buy the place out?" Eli was all smiles for the girl.

Dara was playing it cool. "We got what was on our list," she said, handing out bags. "Hope it's enough."

Fisher nodded. "Should be. If not, we can get Hunter to stop off on the way home to pick up anything missing."

So Hunter wasn't here to run interference between her and Eli. But that didn't matter. No interference was necessary. She could be charming. She could show Eli she wasn't really an evil homewrecker. Well, she could try. She winked at Dara, grabbed the last shopping bag of lights and her art case, and headed toward the trailer.

She worked for two hours. Every time Eli walked by she'd smile or say something funny, but he'd just nod and keep going. Dara joined in, making Eli wander by more often, but still no luck. While she was doing everything in her power to draw Eli out, Dara seemed just as determined to shut the boy down. She hoped Dara wasn't still holding his moodiness against him. She tried to observe the two of them, unobtrusively. Eli was polite, asking to help or to bring the girl a drink. Dara was equally polite, but there was no denying her disinterest. They were too young for this, weren't they?

Preteen romantic drama aside, she and Dara worked hard. They wrapped garland tightly around the four-foot wire frame that would eventually be a topiary rabbit. Once it was suitably green and fluffy looking, they started to unroll lights.

"Looks good." Hunter's voice startled her.

"Well, hello there, stranger." And just like that she was happy. "How was work?" She stood, stretching her back after being hunched over for so long. "How are the puppies?"

"Pups are getting fat, like pups do." He stepped forward, close enough to touch her if he wanted to. And, from the look on his face, he was thinking about more than touching her.

She stepped back, glancing around. She may want him to touch her, but this wasn't the place for it. Eli wasn't glowering at her…yet. "And Mars?" she asked, dropping back to her position beside the lights.

Hunter sat beside her. "She's good. Some movement today."

His nearness complicated her breathing, so she stared at the tangle of lights in her lap.

His voice was low. "You don't want me to kiss you."

She glanced his way, then back at the mess of lights. "No."

He cleared his throat before asking, "No, never again or no, not right now?"

She heard the hesitancy in his voice and met his gaze. "Not right now," she managed to whisper. She wasn't ready to make a public statement with him.

He gave her a quick grin, then asked, "Need help?"

"You should take a break, Miss Stephens," Dara said, taking the lights from her. "I got this. We get volunteer hours."

Josie smiled at Dara. "Okay." The wind kicked up, cutting through her flannel shirt and the thermal underneath. "When did it get cold?"

"Clouds rolled in." Hunter looked up at the sky. "Four years without snow or ice and now we're getting both."

"Guess it followed me from Seattle." She glanced at the sky. "If you're sure you don't need me..."

"Leaving?" he asked, standing beside her.

"No." It took a lot not to hold his hand. "I thought I'd stay awhile and draw. If that's okay?"

"Anytime, Jo. Make yourself at home."

Chapter Ten

No matter what Hunter was doing, he was aware of her. She'd staked out her perfect location on a large willow rocking chair on the corner of his porch, tucked her legs beneath her and opened her sketch pad across her lap. Her presence, her grace, the fluid movement of her pencil back and forth across her sketch pad, fascinated him. Some of her hair had slipped free from her braid and lifted, dancing in the wind, but she didn't bother tucking it into place. She was lost in the world she was creating.

By the time the sun was on the horizon, he was dragging. The float was always an exercise in patience, for the kids and their parents. But in the end nothing smoothed feathers and filled everyone with pride like seeing their work come together. Now that the build was behind them, the mood grew more celebratory.

"I called Gabriel, and he's getting the grill ready," Carol Garcia, one of the moms, said. "Anyone hungry?"

Hunter smiled at the explosion of whistles and yells from the kids. A quick glance at Jo showed she was completely unaware of anything going on around her. He accepted handshakes, offered a few claps on the back, helped locate stray phones or coats, then rounded up any remaining supplies before everyone loaded into their cars and trucks. But Jo kept working.

"Dad?" Eli pulled his coat on, looking more animated than he'd been all day. A glance over his son's shoulder showed Dara climbing into the Garcias' family car. "Greg Hayes wants me to sleep over after the cookout," Eli all but begged.

Hunter looked at his son. He'd been a real handful all day, sullen one minute, smiling and funny the next. He didn't know what to do with him, but he knew keeping Eli home would result in another bout of pouting and he didn't have the energy or the patience for that right now. "Fine. But listen to his folks, remember your manners and don't be too late tomorrow."

Eli nodded, a strange look settling on his face. His son's gaze bounced back and forth between him and Jo. "Okay." His son swallowed before asking, "You gonna come to the cookout for dinner?"

Hunter shook his head. "But you have fun."

Eli's mouth tightened. "See you tomorrow." He shot Jo another look—a look that almost made Hunter call his son back to his side for a talking-to. But he was beginning to wonder if talking to Eli was the answer. This might be a situation Eli should work through on his own.

Hunter nodded at Greg's dad as Eli climbed into the truck. With a nod back, Mr. Hayes and the boys left.

He walked around the trailer, checking wires

and cords, testing the rope tie-downs and tucking extra blankets in. He stood at the edge of the porch and coughed several times, loudly. Jo stretched, arching her back and bending her arms as far back as she could. He watched her come back to reality, slowly, confusion registering as she took in the deserted lawn. "Everyone gone?" she asked. She shivered, turning her big silver-gray gaze toward him.

He nodded. "Didn't want to interrupt you."

"I totally zoned out." She tucked her pens into the small zipper case at her feet. She stood, nodding at the trailer. "That looks amazing."

"You sound like you're surprised." He took the steps two at a time, coming to stand by her on the wooden porch. He turned, surveying the trailer.

"No, not really." She nudged him in the side.

He nudged back. "You were gone today."

She glanced up at him, a slight furrow on her brow. "What do you mean?"

"When you work." He let his gaze wander over

her face; the tip of her nose was red. "The world around you fades away." He knew how it was. The world seemed to fade away whenever they were alone, as they were now.

"Sometimes." Her words were husky, her gaze getting tangled up in his. "Hunter, what are we doing?"

Starting over. But all he said was, "Decorating a float." He knew exactly what she was asking, but he didn't know what she wanted to hear. His fingers tucked a curl behind her ear. "Getting ready for Christmas."

Her voice was unsteady. "Is that all?"

"Is it?"

She shook her head, cupping his face in her hands. "You're not standing here, freezing your butt off, waiting to kiss me?" He smiled, because even though they were completely alone, on several thousand acres, she'd whispered.

His eyes closed, absorbing her touch. "I'll keep waiting, Jo. Until you're ready," he said, daring to meet her gaze. In her eyes, he saw all the need and want and uncertainty that gripped him. He smoothed her hair back from her forehead. "When you're ready, I'll be here."

She leaned into his touch, but her gaze never left his.

"It's cold. Come inside? I've got some stew and corn bread, if you're hungry." He offered her his hand. She could reject him—he sort of expected her to. But he hoped. When it came to Jo, he'd always hope.

She nodded, easing the tension in his stomach. She beamed at him as he held the door open for her. She brushed against him and a whole new range of emotions took over. He watched her, the way her hands twisted in the hem of her shirt, the way her eyes zeroed in on the fire burning low in the grate.

He crossed the room, kneeling before the fire to add some logs and stoke up the flames. When he turned, she stood before him, staring down at him. He stood, aching to drag her against him. If he only knew what she was thinking. "Jo?"

She reached for him, tangling her fingers in his hair and pulling his head to hers. He caught her then, tenderly cradling her face. The sheen in her eyes surprised him, as did the way her lip trembled. "Hunter, please." Her words were husky, rough, needy.

With a growl, every last bit of resistance left him. He'd wanted to be gentle, to love her tenderly, to take time to savor every inch of her. Maybe next time. He bore them back into the wall, nuzzling her neck and ear with his nose.

She smelled like cinnamon, spice and Jo. She ignited every nerve, making his heart ache and his body throb. His lips brushed hers, lingering on her lower lips and making her gasp. He turned into her, sealing her mouth with his. God, he wanted her, he needed her. She stirred a hunger in him that shook him to the core. It was powerful, and relentless.

He nudged her lips open and breathed her in deep. He kissed her then, without restraint. Pure emotion, mingled breaths, his hands cupped her neck, holding her to him. His hand tangled in her hair, tilting her head and holding her, letting his tongue explore until they were both breathless. He ran his nose along her neck, listening to the sound of her ragged breath. She was trembling as his lips latched on to her earlobe.

"Hunter." His name, torn from her lips, set his blood boiling.

He stopped, pulling back. In that moment, he knew there was no one who would ever make him feel the way she did. It was more than her touch, the texture of her skin, her scent. It was Jo. His Jo. In his arms. Where she belonged.

Her eyes opened.

Her hands slipped beneath his shirt, surprising him. She tugged his undershirt free from his jeans, her palms cold enough to make him shiver but not shy away. And then she was kissing his neck, her hands moving over his stomach, his chest, driving him crazy. When she realized his shirt snapped, she yanked, popping it open. Her urgency fueled his—she wanted him and he wasn't going to let her down. He shrugged out of his shirt, ducking down to let her tug his undershirt over his head. She stood there, shaking her head.

"You okay?" he asked.

"It's just… It's you. Different, sure. But you, you know?" She took his hand in hers. "It's still *you*."

Words failed him. She wasn't just talking about his body. She felt it, too? She had to. She blew out a long, unsteady breath.

"I missed you, Jo." His thumb ran over her lower lip. He had to kiss her, had to touch the soft skin beneath her sweater. She was like silk, too fine for the roughened pads of his fingertips. But now that he was touching her, he couldn't stop. He trailed his fingers up her sides, then back down, needing more. "Stay?"

She nodded, taking his hand in hers.

He looked at their joined hands, then led her to his bedroom. He turned, wanting to tell her the truth. He loved her, he wanted her… But before he could say a word, she pulled her sweater off and dropped it on the floor at their feet.

JOSIE GASPED. ONE MINUTE he was staring at her, the next she was lying on her back in his big bed. He leaned over her, the hunger in his eyes inflaming her.

His fingers trailed the edge of her pale blue lace bra. He dipped his head, nuzzling her chest. He pressed soft kisses, the tip of his tongue tracing the valley between her breasts. She clasped his head to her, twisting her fingers in his hair, exhilarating in his touch.

He stood, unhooking his belt and unbuttoning his pants. She rose on her elbows, watching. He raised an eyebrow but didn't say anything. She grinned. She'd been dreaming about Hunter, about his body, about the way he made her feel. Now it was happening and she didn't want to miss a thing.

"Want to help me with my boots?" he asked.

She stood, letting him sit on the edge of the

bed. She turned, tucked his foot between her legs and grabbed the heel of his boot. Then she grabbed the other. She faced him, tossing the boot over her shoulder.

His hands gripped her hips, pulling her between his legs. He buried his face between her breasts, his arms an unbreakable vise about her, holding her, protecting her, loving her. She ran her fingers along his shoulders, arching her back as his mouth nipped at the skin along her bra line.

Her hands traveled along his shoulders. She loved the feel of him, the raw strength of his body.

His fingers fumbled with the clasp of her bra while she shimmied out of her jeans and panties. It had been a long time since she'd stood naked in front of anyone, but the look on his face made her feel beautiful. She was lost to the rasp of his breath, his hands gripping her hips, pulling her against him, skin to skin. His hands were relentless, exploring each curve, stroking and teasing until she thought she would burst.

He kissed her, laying her back on the bed beneath him. At some point his boxers joined the mass of clothes spread out all over his bedroom floor.

She cupped his face, her gaze taking in his every reaction. Flared nostrils, locked jaw, his eyes radiated hunger and need barely restrained. Her fingers trailed along his cheek, his neck, tracing the corded muscle along his sides to grip his hips and arch against him. He groaned, his molten-hot gaze searing her as he slowly entered her. Such sweet torture. Breathing was a challenge. He stopped then, buried deep and breathing hard, and rested his forehead against hers, letting them both adjust to the feel of one another.

His hand smoothed the tangled curls from her face before he kissed her. When he moved, they came together, which drew her into a place of pure sensation. Each touch, each sigh, left her wanting more. She moved with him. She'd forgotten how magic they were together. Sweet and soft, hot and hard, his body pushed her higher. She welcomed each thrust, holding on to him with all the strength she had. When her body tightened, the power of her climax forced her to cry out. His body bowed, each and every muscle contracting against her. Together, they fell over the edge. From raw and unyielding hunger to flushed, peaceful fulfillment, she was content.

He lay at her side, his hand sliding across her stomach to cup her breast. She looked at him. He smiled back. "Warm enough?" he asked gruffly.

She started giggling. "I've still got my socks on."

He sat up, glancing down. "Sexy." He flopped back down beside her.

She shook her head, stroking the side of his face.

His hand covered hers as he leaned down to kiss her.

"Jo…" His face turned serious, worrying her.

She covered his mouth. "Tonight, let's leave the past and the future on the other side of that door." She pointed at his bedroom door. "Please." She hadn't meant for this to happen. Okay, maybe that wasn't entirely true. But now that it had, she didn't know what to do about it. She loved him, she knew that. But saying those three words didn't mean things would simply fall into place. There were complications, lots of complications. She didn't believe in happy endings or forever love stories. And, even if she wanted to believe, she knew she'd mess it up.

And there was Eli.

He was frowning—she could feel it against her palm. "Tell me what's happening at the school. How are the puppies? Mars?" She moved her hand.

"Getting stronger every day." His fingers stroked along the inside of her arm. "How's your dad?"

She closed her eyes to absorb the sensation. "Getting stronger every day."

He chuckled. "He and Lola. You good with that?"

"I'm great with that." She shivered as he drew a finger from the base of her throat to her belly button. "I don't want him alone." She glanced at him. "It's nice to know, no matter where I am, they'll look out for each other."

His hand cupped her breast. "Any decision on the job?"

"Still thinking—" But his mouth on her nipple prevented her from finishing her sentence.

"When do you need to decide?" he asked, looking at her.

"Soon. The job doesn't start till May—"

"Plenty of time to consider all your options." His voice was low, his breath hot against her breast.

"I'll call soon—" she managed to whisper before her nipple was sucked deep into his mouth.

He released her. "I'm hungry."

She blinked, staring at him.

"You hungry?" he asked, smiling a little too smugly.

Food. He was teasing her? Now? Her body was already humming again, but it was a different kind of hunger.

"No?" His fingers trailed across her stomach.

"You're playing with fire, Dr. Boone." She rolled on top of him.

He laughed. "Am I?"

She nodded, aware of his every breath, twitch and reaction. He wasn't as unaffected as he was acting. "You are."

"Jo, you're my kind of fire." His hands came around her, tangling in her hair to pull her face to his.

But before he could kiss her, she pushed off his chest and sat up. "Actually, I could eat." She jumped up before he could grab her.

He sat up and threw a pillow at her. "Mean."

She stuck her tongue out at him. "You started it."

He ran a hand over his head, smiling at her.

"What?"

"You're naked." He wobbled his eyebrows at her. "And damn fine to look at. I'd have to say you're the prettiest thing I've ever seen in my life, Jo Stephens."

Her heart was thumping like crazy, but she said, "You're just hoping you'll get lucky again."

He nodded. "But it's true. Every word of it."

She crossed her arms over her chest, shifting from one sock-covered foot to the other. "I… Th-thank you," she stuttered. "I— Let's eat?"

He stood up then, all glorious manliness, and it was her turn to stare.

"Here." He tossed her his undershirt.

She smiled and tugged it on. She rolled up the sleeves, hugging herself and sighing at the intoxicating scent of Hunter.

He pulled on his boxer shorts and his flannel snap-up shirt. "Stew?"

"Stew."

They warmed up two big bowls of stew and a

plate of honey corn bread, carrying it back into the living room to picnic before the fireplace.

"Yummy," she said between bites.

"Cooking." He held up the bowl. "One of the many skills I hadn't planned on picking up."

"Cooking is a good skill to have."

"I didn't want Eli to grow up on frozen dinners or scrambled eggs. I used my mom's cookbook a lot, in the beginning." He took a long drink of water. "Can't touch her cooking, but we don't starve."

She grinned, imagining Hunter poring over cookbooks and meticulously following each recipe. He was a scientist, methodical and calculating. She had no doubt he'd spent hours making sure he'd done his mom's recipes proud. Unlike Josie's mother, Mags Boone was one of those women who excelled at motherhood. She had died in a car accident a year after Josie had gone to New Mexico. Josie had come back for the funeral—she'd had to. Seeing Hunter so sad, the Boone family so uncertain, had been a nightmare. So was seeing Amy with Hunter's tiny son. She'd given each of them her sincere condolences and headed back to the safety of school. But she'd often thought about Hunter and the family, written countless letters and emails she never sent. Nothing she could say would ease the ache of Mags passing.

"I bet she would've loved that you cook her food for Eli." Josie beamed at him, loving his answering smile. "What's another skill you never thought you'd learn?"

Hunter sat back against the couch, his long legs stretched out in front of him. He stared into the fire. "Well…potty training." He laughed. "I mean, I was planning on helping out. I just thought it'd be a team effort."

Josie sat her bowl on the floor at her side. "When did Amy leave?"

Hunter looked at her. "We lived under the same roof for a little over a year. Then she went back on the rodeo circuit, stopping in now and then."

"B-but Eli was a baby." She couldn't imagine leaving something so little and helpless. "You… How… Wow." She took his hand in hers. "So, you were in school with a baby, on your own."

He shook his head. "I was never on my own, Jo. My father, my brothers, Renata, hell, my aunts came down to help out whenever they could."

She nodded. "I know. It's just—"

"He never had a mother." He squeezed her hand. "You know all about that."

She scooted across the floor to snuggle against his chest. "Oh, I have a mother. She's on husband number seven. But this is the second time she's married this one, so maybe he'll be a keeper."

Hunter's laugh was low. "You like him?"

"I don't know him, really. They came up when I had a show in Montesano last year. He seemed nice enough. He's younger, of course, but he loves her." She shrugged. "I think."

"What about you?" he asked. "Learned any skills you never thought you'd learn?"

"Where do I start?" She sighed. "Changing a tire and my oil—it's cheaper than having everything serviced. Once a mechanic finds out you're a single woman, they see dollar signs. Minor plumbing repairs and electrical repairs."

"Cooking, too?"

She smiled up at him. "Cooking for one is boring."

He frowned. "Why one?"

She swallowed. "I was almost engaged. But I just couldn't do it."

"What did he do?" His voice was gruff, angry.

"He didn't do a thing. He was a really nice guy. He still is a really nice guy."

"You're still involved?"

"If I was, this wouldn't have happened." She shot him a look. "He'd like to be, but nothing's changed."

"Then what happened?"

She sat up, reaching for her glass of water. She

didn't know what to say, exactly. "It's me. I'm not wired that way. The marrying way, I mean. If I was, Wes would be a good husband. He's this sweet, supportive, funny guy who loves me. But I didn't love him that way." She swirled her water glass, staring into the fire. She didn't really want to talk about Wes... She didn't know how long they'd have time like this together. She glanced at Hunter to find him watching her.

Hunter took the glass from her. "You're too hard on yourself, Jo."

She frowned. She wasn't hard on herself—she just accepted her limitations. Not that looking at Hunter, all ruffled and manly, didn't make her wish she was another kind of woman. A true-blue veterinarian cowboy's wife type of woman...

He lowered his head, his mouth latching on to hers with a passion that startled her. His hand slipped under the edge of her shirt, gripping her hip. When his tongue traced the seam of her lips, she inched closer. Not close enough. She loved his soft groan, the hitch in his breath, as she straddled him.

"Still hungry?" she asked, nipping his bottom lip.

"Yes, ma'am," he rasped. "For dessert."

Chapter Eleven

Morning sunlight spilled into the bedroom, waking Josie with a start. She lay there, staring at the aged wood beams running across the ceiling. She was here, really here. And Hunter was snoring softly beside her. She grinned, turning her head on the down-filled pillow. His features were peaceful when he slept. She stared at him, torn. She wanted to stay. She wanted to run her fingers over the stubble on his chin. She wanted to wake him up and make love to him again. She wanted to talk about possibilities. And that terrified her.

Nothing had been said last night because she'd

told him not to say anything. Doubt reared its ugly head.

Maybe nothing had been said because neither of them wanted to go *there*.

Yes, they were attracted to each other. They had a history and they liked each other. But a future for them couldn't be that easy. She and Hunter had a complicated relationship. Another thing her mother had warned her away from: complications. Complications led to distractions, which led to disinterest, and being left.

So words like *possibilities* and *relationships* shouldn't come into play, for both their sakes. Instead, last night was…the best mistake of her life. An amazing, magical, earth-shattering, mind-blowing mistake. She needed to end this now before she let her stupid heart convince her otherwise.

They weren't kids anymore. Other people would get hurt—like Eli. Eli, who might be home at any minute.

She lay there a second longer, memorizing everything about Hunter. She couldn't let him in. She couldn't love him. Her hand hovered over his cheek, itching to touch him.

The cold, hard truth was too big to ignore. It was too late. She did love him—she always had. The trick would be leaving without making things even more complicated than they already were. He could never know how she felt and she needed to get a grip on her out-of-control libido.

First step: getting out of his bed. She slipped from the bed, then spent a good ten minutes finding her clothes. No matter how hard she searched, one sock was missing. She dressed as quietly as possible, tugged her hair into a sloppy ponytail and eased from his bedroom.

She made it to the front door when his growl of a question made her jump. "Where are you going?" He was all sleep-rumpled, bleary-eyed and shirtless.

"Home," she whispered, even though there was no reason to do so.

"You weren't going to say goodbye?" He frowned.

"You were asleep." As far as excuses went, she knew it was lame. From the disappointment on his face, he knew it was lame, too. "I...I didn't want to wake you up."

"You wanted me to wake up alone?" His long stride erased the space between them. His expression was confused and, maybe, a little sad. "Why are you running out on me?"

She blinked, shaking her head. "I'm not—"

"Stop, Jo." His hands clasped her upper arms. "Let's have some coffee and talk."

"Hunter," she said, "my dad—"

His hands slipped from her shoulders as he stepped back. "Admit you're scared. But don't use your dad as an excuse to avoid talking to me."

Her first instinct was to fight. The only problem with that? He was right, that's exactly what she was doing—and feeling. Which meant arguing with him was stupid. But talking to him, actually talking about feelings, would be bad. Especially now that she knew she loved him. What if he asked her how she felt? What if he loved her?

Joy and anticipation and pure, unfiltered panic pressed in on her, forcing the air from her lungs. Leaving was the best option, for both of them. She glanced at the door two steps away, the doorknob within easy reach.

"I don't want another eleven years of silence, Jo." His words were so raw, so hard, she had to look at him. Pain filled his eyes, so deep she was drowning in it. "Whatever you say can't be as bad as saying nothing."

She couldn't look away, no matter how much she wanted to. It killed her, to see him hurting. "I don't know what you want me to say."

He sighed, rubbing a hand over his face. "Why are you leaving?"

She shook her head, then shrugged. "I…I'm not good at the whole one-night-stand thing." She heard how callous her words were.

He was scowling now. "That's not what this is."

She couldn't stop the words from coming. "What is it? What is this?" She pointed back and forth between the two of them. "Hunter…" Her voice broke. *Damn it.* She didn't want this. Her heart might be a traitor, but she wasn't going to give in. She wasn't.

His hand cupped her cheek. "Would falling in love be that bad?" Why did he have to look at her like that? With tenderness and hope. Hope, which led to disappointment, disillusionment and heartbreak.

"Yes," she rasped. "It would be a mistake. A huge mistake. Like last night…all of this." She was spiraling out of control—she could hear it in her voice.

His gaze was relentless, searching and intense, while his thumb stroked along her cheekbone. She tried not to shudder, she did, but she failed. His posture changed, and he relaxed. His crooked smile appeared, and one brow arched as he leaned forward. "People make mistakes in life—it happens all the time." His hand grasped her chin, tilting her head back. "Loving you isn't one of them."

Was he saying he loved her? Now? Was the room spinning? And he was kissing her... Holding her in a way that told her he'd never let her go. How could she be so happy and so miserable at the same time?

"Stay, Jo," he murmured against her lips.

"I can't." She pressed against his chest.

"You can. If you weren't so stubborn, you'd see that."

"Always have been—" She sucked in a deep breath, hoping to shake off the all-too-tempting invitation his lips were issuing as they traveled along her neck. "Stubborn," she whispered.

His laugh was low, his breath warm on her skin. "It's hot as hell," he murmured, lightly biting her earlobe.

She gasped. If she didn't push out of his hold now, she'd be pushing him back into the bedroom. Pulling away was hard, a lot harder than she wanted to admit. She was still a little breathless when she said, "You don't play fair."

He smoothed her hair from her face. "All's fair in love and war. Can't help it if I get you all hot and bothered." He shrugged, his smile fading. "I can't make you stay, if you're set on going."

"I am." She nodded, trying to convince them both.

"Then go." His hand rested at the base of her neck, his thumb resting in the hollow of her throat. She swallowed, his touch a brand against her flesh. He grinned, his thumb stroking her neck. "I'll see you at my dad's later for dinner."

She scowled at him, then yanked the door open and stepped out onto the front porch. She ignored him, and his laughter, as she walked out. He followed her, just to poke at her, she knew. It was cold and he was wearing his boxers and not much else. She was about to point that out to him, when someone cleared their throat. A woman stood, her arm resting on the hood of a big shiny four-door pickup truck.

Not just any woman. *Amy*. Not that Amy even looked at her—her brown eyes were glued on Hunter. She stepped forward, blond hair swinging, all sass and attitude. "Are you kidding me?"

"Amy?" The look on Hunter's face told Josie he wasn't expecting his ex-wife any more than she was.

Amy laughed, a hard, angry sound. "Talk about a homecoming."

Hunter's calm was surprising. "What are you doing here?"

"Eli called and asked me to come home." She tossed her head back, her hands resting on her hips. She'd kept in shape—her skintight jeans and plunging neckline made that clear. "So, I did. It's Christmas and all. But I'm guessing you weren't expecting me. Or maybe you were. Maybe you knew I was on my way." She leveled Josie with a glare so hostile there was no mistaking her implication.

Whatever Amy was thinking, it wasn't pretty. Josie had never been on the receiving end of

such unfiltered aggression. Amy might be looking for a fight, but that was the last thing she
needed. Eli disliked her now, but he would really
hate her if she went toe-to-toe with his mother.
"I was just leaving," Josie muttered.

"I sure as hell hope Eli isn't home." Amy put
her hands on her hips. "A boy his age doesn't
need to see his dad sleeping around."

"Are you serious?" Hunter's tone was hard.

"Hell, yes, I am. Where is he? Where's our
son?" Josie heard Amy stress *our son*—it was
impossible not to hear it. As if she needed to be
reminded that Eli was their son.

"He's sleeping over at Greg's," Josie said.

Amy's nostrils flared, her eyes narrowed.
"Was I talking to *you*? Did I ask *you* where my
son was?" She stepped forward, fists clenched.

"Amy, that's enough," Hunter said. "This is
my place—"

"Where *my* son lives," Amy argued. "I don't
give a shit about who you're sleeping with. But
her? I know Eli has a problem with her. You

know it, too. You might not give a rat's ass about your son's feelings, but I sure as hell do."

"You really want to go there?" Hunter's voice was deceptively soft.

Amy's eyes went round, her lips thin and pinched. She didn't say a word, but it was hard for her, Josie could tell.

"I think you need to leave." Hunter crossed his arms over his chest. "Now."

Josie glanced at Hunter, torn. Amy was laying it on thick, but she wasn't entirely wrong. And they all knew it. Hunter must have guessed what she was thinking, because he frowned and shook his head. "Jo—"

"I'm going to be late," Josie said, stepping blindly around Amy and hurrying to the barn. It was one of the longest walks she'd ever made. Her heart echoed in her ears with each step, and her eyes burned from the tears choking her.

She heard Hunter call after her, but ignored it. She couldn't stop. Not with Amy primed for battle, screaming at Hunter. "What the hell is the matter with you? You bring that woman here, into Eli's home? After everything—"

Hunter's voice was too low to make out, not that she wanted to hear their conversation. Instead, she walked faster. What was she doing? What had she been thinking? What if Eli had come home last night? He would have been devastated to find her there. And his relationship with his father would have suffered for it.

She fumbled with her keys, trying to unlock her door, but dropped them instead. She knelt quickly, reaching for them, slipped on the dew-slicked grass and ended up on her knees. She sat, leaning against the car and staring up at the pale blue sky. The wind whipped her curls around her face and stung her eyes, making it okay for her to cry—a little. She sniffed, hugging her knees to her chest.

How many years had she spent avoiding complications? How many opportunities had she passed up because she didn't want pain? When she'd left Stonewall Crossing, she'd been testing

Hunter. She knew that now. Was it fair? No. Had she set him up for failure? Maybe. She knew what a catch he was. Amy wasn't the only one waiting to swoop in when she wasn't around. But she'd gone, anyway. And life, in all its complete misery, had eventually moved on. She had moved on. Sort of. Her attention followed a stray cloud across the blue sky.

She'd never stopped loving him. And that one, stupid emotion was the reason everything was falling apart. All those years of proving she wasn't her mother, only to act exactly like her. Following her heart, regardless of the consequences to everyone else.

"Jo?" Hunter's voice was soft. He stood, jeans unbuttoned and shoved into his boots, shirt flapping wide enough to reveal every gorgeous ridge and dip of his muscular chest and stomach.

She almost groaned in frustration, angrily wiping the stray tears from her cheeks. "I dropped my keys." She pushed up, turning to unlock the door.

"You locked your car? Out here?" His hand came around, taking the keys.

She wouldn't face him. Instead, she held her hand out. "Keys."

"Nope."

She clenched her fist, then opened it again. "Keys!" She waited, and waited, but he didn't say a word or give her the keys. She spun around, all restraint gone. "Give me the keys," she hissed.

He tucked the keys in his pocket. "In a minute." He grabbed her shoulders, pulling her against him. "Don't leave like this."

"Like what?" Why did he have to smell so good?

He held her so tightly she couldn't push him away. "Thinking this is wrong. Amy's wrong."

"Eli hates me."

"He doesn't hate you." He sighed. "Look at me, please."

She stared at his chest. It was hard, covered in the lightest dusting of hair, coarse beneath her fingers. She swallowed, staring at his neck instead. The strong, sun-kissed neck she'd enjoying kissing not too many hours ago.

"Amy is part of my life—she always will be. I can't say I'm happy about that, but it's the truth." He paused. "But I *want* you in my life, Jo. To stay, here, with me and Eli."

She stared up at him. "But Eli—"

"Is my son. It might take some time, but he'll come 'round. He wants me to be happy." He kissed her forehead. "And, damn, Jo, you make me happy. Always have."

She felt the tears building then, hating the weakness they showed. This was bad. He was saying everything she wanted to hear, everything she'd dreamed he'd say. But it wasn't enough.

She'd never completely gotten over the hurt her mother had caused, never forgotten how it felt to be passed over for her mom's happiness. She'd resented all the men in her mother's life and held them at arm's length because she knew they weren't there to stay. In time, she'd come to terms with the choices her mom had made, but she'd never forgotten how betrayed she'd felt. She, who was always there to love and support her mother, didn't make her mother happy. The thought of Eli feeling that way about the father he adored was too much. "I can't."

The range of emotions that crossed his face was quick, but she soaked in every spellbinding expression. "Yes, you can." His determination was clear. "And this time, I'm not gonna let you go without a fight. You hear me?"

She shook her head, forcing the pure joy his words stirred deep down inside her. She drew in a deep breath and spoke carefully. "There's no fight. Last night was amazing, no denying that." She cleared her throat, her heart rebelling against the next words she forced out. "But this isn't where I want to be, Hunter. This isn't my life."

His hold lessened on her the slightest bit. "You keep telling yourself that, Jo. I'm happy to prove you wrong." He pressed a kiss to her forehead before he released her, leaving her unsteady on her own two feet. He unlocked the car door, held it open for her and handed her the keys when she was sitting inside. She hadn't realized how cold she was until she was out of the morning wind.

And there he stood, basically shirtless, smiling at her like that. She could see his breath on the air. He had to be freezing. "Get inside before you catch a cold," she snapped.

He laughed. "Yes, ma'am."

She shook her head, scowling at him until she was pulling down the driveway. Glancing back provided her with instantaneous relief. Amy and her big red truck weren't parked in front of the house. Not that she had any right to feel one way or the other about Amy being there. Hunter had told her the truth, as far as he was concerned. And what he'd said... All sorts of ridiculous and conflicting emotions warred inside her. Tears were streaming down her face, some happy, some not so happy.

Chapter Twelve

Josie made sure each loaf of sweet bread was wrapped in waxed paper, then tin foil, before packing them into the plastic travel container. "Are you ready?" she called out to her father.

"In a minute," he answered. "Still can't believe your car broke down last night. You need to let the rental car people know. Maybe you can get your money back."

"Sure, Dad. I'll do that," she said quickly, hating lying to her dad. Sprinkles, who'd been watching her from the doorway, yapped at her. "What?" she asked. Sprinkles cocked her head to one side, making a strange little growl. Of disapproval? Did the dog know she was lying?

She put her hands on her hips and frowned at the dog. "Give me a break, Sprinkles," she whispered. The dog yapped again. "I am not going to tell him I had a…sleepover at Hunter's place. And I'm not going to let something that eats my face cream make me feel guilt." She turned her back on the dog and straightened up the kitchen.

Why did staying with her father make her feel as if she needed to sneak around? He'd made no secret that he wanted her to give it another chance with Hunter. Heck, her dad would probably throw them a party. Maybe that was why she didn't say anything. In the twelve hours since her night with Hunter, she'd felt more at odds than ever.

"Everything packed up?" Her father peeked into the kitchen. "Can you feed Sprinkles for me?"

"If you'll hurry up." She shot a pointed look at the shaving cream on his face. "Lola will be here any second."

"We're picking her up," her father said, returning to the bathroom. "Awfully eager to get there, aren't we?"

She didn't answer. She *was* eager. She wanted to see Hunter and Eli. Tonight was an opportunity to pretend she was part of that family. She hung up her apron and flipped off the kitchen lights. The dog was still sitting in the doorway. "Is that what this stare-down is about? Are you hungry, Sprinkles? Sorry, I'm still not fluent in dog speak yet."

Sprinkles did her little growl-yip thing. Josie chuckled.

It took an hour to get ready. Her father had changed shirts six times and nicked himself while shaving. She'd picked out a new shirt, located a Band-Aid and fielded several phone calls concerning the Gingerbread Festival while trying to lure the stubborn little terrier into the kitchen for dinner.

"She likes to eat in the dining room, like me," her father explained after Josie had circled the kitchen table for the fifth time.

"Really, Dad? But you're not eating in the dining room, so why can't she just be a dog and eat in the kitchen?" Josie put her hands on her hips. Sprinkles circled her, yipping loudly. "Am I supposed to set you a place at the table? Or will you have your meal on the floor?"

Her father frowned at her. "Don't get all sassy. A man gets lonely without a companion." A strange look crossed his face and he patted his shirt pocket. "Be right back." He moved, more quickly than she'd seen him move in a while, back down the hall to his room.

Josie poured Sprinkles a heaping bowl of dog food, then refilled her water bowl. "What, no thank-you?" Sprinkles eyed the food, then the water, then flopped down in her dog bed. Josie shook her head and loaded the food they were bringing into her father's small extended cab pickup truck. Her father came out, looking rather dashing.

"You look all spiffed up, Dad." She noticed the

slight color on his cheeks. "So, how was bingo last night?"

"Oh, fine. Lola won, as always. I'm convinced she's got the game rigged." He locked the front door behind them.

"By using magnetized bingo balls or something?" Josie couldn't help but tease as she climbed into the truck.

Her father joined her, staring at her. "I never thought of that one. Hmm, sounds like a lot of work—"

"Dad, I was kidding." She laughed.

"You sure we made enough?" Her father eyed the six loaves of sweet bread and tray of assorted delectable holiday treats. "There are a lot of Boones out there."

"I think we'll be fine, Dad."

"You should see Fisher eat. And Eli. Boys must have hollow legs."

They picked up Lola, and Josie moved to the backseat, listening to them chatter about the upcoming festivities on the square and any little snippets of gossip Lola had to share, as well.

"I know she's a friend of yours, but there's a rumor that Principal Upton has herself a fella." Lola turned in her seat.

Josie shook her head. "Not that I know of. Annabeth's been pretty up-front about being lonely." She didn't mention the sexting to Lola. She might adore the older woman, but she knew Lola Worley loved to talk. "Out of curiosity, why?"

Lola nodded. "Well, her neighbor saw flowers being delivered to her house. And she's had a babysitter three more times than she usually does."

Josie didn't say a word. One of those nights, Annabeth had been with her. And she'd had Career Night, too. But that was all she knew of. She sighed. Was she really going to dissect Annabeth's babysitting schedule to determine whether she was dating? No. No, she wasn't.

And she wasn't going to ask her, either. If Annabeth wanted to tell her, she would.

The closer they got to Boone Ranch, the more nervous Josie felt. Once they parked, she took more time than necessary collecting the travel containers of food. Her dad and Lola were inside when she heard, "Can I help?"

Hunter pulled her against him, his hands sliding down the length of her back to her hips and back up to rest on her shoulders.

SHE FELT SO good against him. As though she was made for him.

"Hi." Her whisper was unsteady. He liked it.

He nodded, bending to kiss her.

"Hunter—"

"Hold that thought," he murmured, pressing his lips against hers. It was one of those deep, openmouthed, soft kisses that had her clinging to his shirt and swaying into him. With a soft groan, he loosened his hold on her. As tempting as it was to load her into his truck and take her to his place, he knew better. Instead, he dropped a swift kiss on the tip of her nose, asking, "What were you saying?"

Her breathless laugh warmed him through. "I think I was going to say something about being seen or this wasn't a good idea..." She trailed off.

"That's what I thought."

"You knew I was going to say that? And you kissed me?" He watched her eyes narrow.

"Worked for me," he argued, collecting the containers from the truck. "Good thing it's cold out here or everyone in the house would know I was hungry for something other than food right now."

She stared up at him. Something about ruffling her feathers made him a little too happy. He winked. "Come on. We stay out here too long, Lola will talk."

She hurried up the steps to the porch, holding open the door for him.

"Happy holidays!" His father was all smiles,

giving Jo a big hug and kiss. "You look as pretty as one of your pictures."

Hunter disagreed. Pretty didn't begin to describe how Jo looked. Her black sweater fitted her snugly, hugging her breasts and reminding him of how well they fit in his hands.

"Aren't your pictures normally animals?" Fisher picked her up in a bear hug. "Or landscapes? Don't be offended, Josie."

"Hi, Fisher." She laughed. "You really don't have to pick me up every time we see each other."

"No?" his brother asked.

"No," Hunter answered before he thought.

His brother grinned, ear to ear, as he set her down. "Looks like he can't stand a little competition, Josie," Fisher whispered, winking at her.

Hunter ignored his brother's teasing, but not the rosy hue of Josie's cheeks. If he didn't get a grip on his emotions, tonight was going to be one hell of a long night.

"Joselyn." Archer nodded at her. "Nice to see you."

"You, too, Archer." She smiled in response, her nerves showing.

Ryder winked in greeting, and she waved back.

"Hey, Josie." His sister, Renata, was all smiles.

Josie stared at Renata before pulling her into a hug. "God, you're gorgeous."

He grinned. His little sister was a little too gorgeous for his liking. Too blonde, too blue-eyed, with a figure that turned too many heads. Thank God she had a good head on her shoulders or he and his brothers would be headed for trouble.

"She's all grown up," his father agreed.

Renata laughed, hugging her back. "It has been a while since we've seen each other."

"Time goes faster the older you are." His father hooked arms with Josie. "That's why it's so important to make every minute count."

"You sound like my dad," Josie said.

"Imparting words of wisdom is a father's job." Teddy patted Josie's arm. "Come say hello, Eli.

We've got guests, so pretend like you've got some manners." He winked at his grandson.

Hunter had never had to punish his son before, not really, but Eli had never treated anyone with such disrespect. He barely nodded at Jo, before shaking hands with Carl and letting Lola kiss his cheek.

"Santa's big on manners." Renata poked Eli in the side, making Eli smile reluctantly.

Dinner was a mash-up of good and bad. Hunter sat beside Josie, enjoying every accidental brush of her hand against his. When he passed the rolls or the butter, he let his fingers linger just so he could watch her cheeks turn rosy. He couldn't resist touching her. The way her breath caught in her throat when he let his hand fall from his lap to her thigh almost had him dragging her from the room. She shifted to the opposite side of her chair, her grip on her wineglass tightening. He couldn't stop grinning. He couldn't ignore the pull between them. Electric, hot, charging the air between them. Damn, but he was hard with want before they'd started eating.

Conversation ebbed and flowed, but every second he was aware of her. The way she looked at her father and Lola was so hopeful and happy. The longing on her face as she laughed at his siblings' teasing… She hadn't had a lot of family get-togethers and love in her home growing up. He knew her mom had done a number on her, muddying the waters when it came to real love and commitment. And his betrayal, with Amy, hadn't helped. But, if she'd give him another chance, he'd show her that family could be loyal, sticking together to the end, even when things were tough.

Josie stiffened, her entire body rigid.

"Jo?" he whispered, the others engrossed in one of Fisher's stories.

She looked at him, her silver-gray eyes searching his.

"You okay?" he asked.

"Fine." But he heard the tremor in her voice.

"You can write a book about that," Fisher finished. "Not sure it's fit for kids, though."

Hunter had no idea what his brother had been saying, but he smiled. "Don't think so."

Fisher shrugged.

"When are you leaving?" Eli asked.

Hunter stared at his son. So did everyone else at the table.

"I...I mean," the boy stuttered, seeing his mistake, "you're going back to Washington, right, Miss Stephens?"

Hunter was stunned. And more than a little hurt. What had he done to make his son worry so? To think Eli would be replaced by anyone in his heart? It pissed Hunter off that his son was talking to Jo like that. But there was something else going on with Eli, and he needed to find out what it was—soon.

"I'm trying to convince her to stay," her father said. "Seems to me, she can write anywhere."

"And all her stories are about Stonewall Crossing, anyway," Lola chimed in. "I've got that little stone cottage needing a tenant."

"Any news about the university job?" his father asked.

"I told them I'd get back to them in January," she admitted. "There's a chance for me to do a lovely in memoriam mural at the vet school I'd really love to do before I go."

"You're staying?" Eli's voice was tight.

"No." Josie shook her head. Pain laced Eli's words. Hunter heard it, and Jo heard it, too. There was no doubt how his son felt about Jo, about Jo being a part of their life. "Eli, I'm... I have no plans to stay." Hunter looked at her, wanting to argue. But she didn't look at him— she was too busy watching Eli. Her sadness twisted his heart. His son's rigid jaw, the way he stared at his empty plate, all but ripped Hunter's heart right out.

A heavy, awkward silence descended.

"Dessert?" Renata asked.

"I'll help clear." Jo jumped up, a smile pasted

on her face. She made her way around the table, collecting plates, before disappearing into the kitchen with Renata.

A few minutes later, Renata appeared with a pie in one hand and a large platter of cookies in the other. But no Jo. He waited another five minutes before he headed for the kitchen. Jo's sleeves were pushed up, her hands submerged in a sink full of soap suds and dinner dishes. She scrubbed each dish, attacking it until Hunter knew they didn't need to be run through the dishwasher. She loaded them in anyway, her movements jerky and stiff. When all the dishes were loaded, she scrubbed down the counter and tidied up. He watched her pull in a deep, shaky breath. Was there anything he could say to her? Any way to convince her that their love was worth the trouble? Her eyes went round when she turned to find him leaning against the doorway.

"Feel better?" he asked, not moving.

She shook her head.

He almost crossed to her, almost took her in his arms. But she held herself so rigidly he was afraid he'd break her. "He's a kid, Jo."

"A kid that doesn't like me much." She smoothed her black sweater.

She was hurting. And vulnerable. "I *like* you enough for both of us." His gaze held hers, willing her to see things his way.

"Dad." Eli squeezed between his father and the door. "Grandpa Teddy wants you."

"Okay." He paused, looking at his son, then Jo. "Help Jo make the coffee. She doesn't know her way around the kitchen."

He didn't know who was angrier, Eli or Jo. But damn it, his son needed to know Jo for the woman she was, not the monster Amy had made her out to be. He gave Jo a wink, leveled a warning at his son and left.

Chapter Thirteen

Eli glanced at her, wary, before opening the kitchen cabinets. No point in ignoring him. She could try to talk to him. Hunter obviously thought it was a good idea. "So, Eli," she began, speaking to his back. He didn't turn around or acknowledge her, but she kept going. "The float looks great. You happy with it?"

He shrugged but didn't turn around.

"You do this every year?" She plugged in the coffeepot, filling it with water. "The club, I mean."

He nodded, putting mugs on the counter.

She paused, swallowing back her sigh. Well,

this was going well. "Can you point me in the direction of the coffee?"

He opened another cabinet and pulled out a large container of coffee. He set it on the counter beside her, without looking at her, or saying a word.

"Thank you." She added several scoops of coffee, searching for some way to crack his armor. She glanced at the boy, an idea taking shape. She knew she was playing dirty, but she was getting desperate. "How long has Dara lived in Stonewall Crossing? I get the impression she's new."

He glanced at her. "She just moved here."

"I thought so." She watched the coffee brewing, trying not to react to the fact that he was talking to her. "She's still learning the town, asking lots of questions. She's been such a help at the bakery."

"She's been working at the bakery?" he asked.

Josie nodded. "I'd been talking to Miss Worley about how much work it is, with Dad's injury and all, and she volunteered. She's a solid baker, but she loves the decorating part. I think her cookies are the prettiest in the shop."

"She's artsy. Real creative." He stopped, turning one of the mugs around in his hands. "Still need help?"

Josie couldn't hide her surprise. "Really?" He must really like Dara, to offer his help to her. "S-sure." In case he didn't know, she added, "I... I'll be there, too, you know?"

"Yeah." For a split second he wasn't fuming. His blue-green eyes assessed her carefully before he frowned. He sounded a little sad, a little irritated, when he said, "But my dad won't be." He was watching her, as if he was waiting for something.

She didn't really know what to say, so she murmured, "Oh."

Renata swept into the kitchen, eyeing them both before asking, "Coffee ready? Eli, where are the trays? We can't go back and forth with everything." She paused. "Wow, Josie, did you clean up? It looks great, thanks."

"Of course," she said. "It's the least I can do after the lovely dinner. Your dad's quite the cook."

"I guess that's what single men do—learn to cook." Renata smiled. "My dad, your dad, all of my brothers. Well, not Ryder. But he's really good about visiting right at dinnertime so he never goes hungry." She put the sugar pot on the tray, then pulled out a small pitcher and some milk. "Hunter's the best cook, after my dad. Guess he's got more than himself to feed." Renata nudged her nephew, earning her a smile from Eli.

When she carried the coffee into the living room, conversation was in full swing. Hunter was sitting at one end of a long leather couch, with enough room for her to sit beside him. And as much as she wanted to sit there and sink into his side, she didn't. Instead, she perched on a small stool in front of the roaring fireplace, taking care not to look at Hunter or the inviting spot beside him.

"I don't care what the zoo official says." Archer was shaking his head. "I'm sick and tired of the excuses. Bottom line is they don't want the cheetah, even if she is rehabilitated."

"But why?" Lola asked. "I don't understand, Archer."

"Money's tight, funding is hard to come by, and she's one more mouth to feed and body to vaccinate."

"What will you do?" Josie asked, doctoring her coffee with extra sugar. "Can you keep her?"

Archer shrugged. "It's not like the preserve is flush with extra funds. But I'll figure something out."

Fisher was talking then, but Josie let her attention wander. The years had been good to the Boone family.

She studied Archer Boone. He'd always been a serious sort, even as a boy. His brothers were tall, thick and broad. But Archer was taller, lean and trim. Her gaze traveled to Fisher, sprawled in an armchair, devouring cookies. He was the thickest, a tree trunk of a man. He'd been the smallest as a boy. But, no matter how much his physique might have changed, he was still the joker she remembered. Now, Ryder... She had to bite back a smile, remembering Annabeth's undisguised lust for the youngest Boone brother. There was no doubt Ryder was probably the best looking, and he knew it. But there was also no question he was trouble.

When she finally allowed herself to look at Hunter, he cocked an eyebrow at her. She smiled, holding her mug in front of her mouth. The slight tilt of his head, the quirk of his mouth... She loved him. And it felt wonderful and warm and horribly painful. His brow furrowed before she turned away, staring into her mug to collect herself.

What was she doing, sitting here, daydreaming? Never in her wildest dreams had she thought she'd be in Stonewall Crossing having dinner with the Boones, talking animals and family, a week before Christmas.

"We should be getting on home," her father said. "It's getting late and tomorrow's going to be crazy. And we still have to get Miss Lola home."

Did her dad just wink at Lola? She glanced at Hunter, and he was smiling from ear to ear.

"Everything's ready, Carl, don't fret." Lola patted her father's hand. "Between Josie, Dara and me, we've made an army of cookies, and then some. Unless Fisher's eaten them all, that is." Lola shook her head as Fisher ate another gingerbread man in two bites.

Fisher grinned. "They're good."

"Obviously." Renata smirked. "Chamber's ready, too. Of course, everyone's a little too excited about the reporter coming from the State Tourism Department. We want Stonewall Crossing to shine as a tourist destination. And a safe place to get an exceptional education." She smiled at her brothers.

"Exciting times," Lola said.

"Nice for our little piece of heaven to get such

positive attention," Teddy Boone added, sipping his coffee.

Ryder was clearly unimpressed. He shot Josie a look, then rolled his eyes. Maybe the youngest Boone wasn't as content with life as the rest of them appeared to be.

"You might be just a little bit biased, Daddy." Renata kissed her father's cheek.

"What time does everything start up tomorrow?" Josie asked, standing. "Do I need to do anything?"

"I'll come get you around three. They start lining up for the parade pretty soon after that." Hunter stood, moving to her side. "Thought maybe we could walk around the square afterward. Carolers. Hot chocolate. That sort of thing."

It would be all too easy to get lost in his blue-green eyes, to forget Eli and Amy and how terrified she was of commitment. Especially when he was looking at her like that, as if she was the only woman in the world. Not caring that they had a room full of observers, his son included.

"I— You'll be too busy, won't you?" Her voice was a little unsteady. "Taking the float apart?"

"It can wait. Times like tomorrow don't come very often." He took her hand in his. "It's important to make every minute count."

"Damn right," Teddy Boone said.

Hunter knew exactly what he was doing. No way he was going to let her leave without making it plain to everyone what his intentions were.

The look on her face almost broke his resolve to take things slow. Holding her hand was one thing—wrapping her up in a kiss that claimed her would be something else. But the surprise on her face and the pleasure that creased the corners of her eyes were tempting, very tempting.

"What do you say, Jo?" he asked, squeezing her hand.

Her nod was slow. "I'd love to."

She looked so pretty he had to fist his hand to

keep from reaching for her. "I'll help you load things up."

He ignored the expressions of everyone in the room. He knew Carl and his father were tickled pink. Fisher and Lola, too, undoubtedly. Ryder and Archer wouldn't care. Renata…well, she was worried about him. She'd told him to take things slow, to keep a rein on his heart. As if that was ever a possibility when it came to Jo.

And Eli? He looked at his son and smiled. His boy needed to know that Jo made him happy, that holding her hand meant smiling. Eli was red-faced, angry tears in his accusing eyes.

Hunter walked by, refusing to cave. He helped Josie get everything loaded into Carl's truck, waiting as everyone said their goodbyes before helping Lola into the cab and dropping a swift kiss on Jo's cheek.

"Hunter—" The worry in her voice stopped him.

"I'll talk to him, Jo." His hand cupped her cheek. "I'll see you tomorrow."

"I don't want to cause problems, Hunter. I—"

"You're not." He smiled. "I'll figure it out."

She didn't look convinced as he loaded her into her father's truck. He watched the taillights until they'd faded into the black night. He stood a little longer, letting the crickets chirp and the wind calm him before heading back into the house.

He loaded Eli into his truck ten minutes later. His son didn't say a word as they drove, but his hands were clenched in his lap, his head turned away.

Hunter let it go until they were home. He needed the time to think through what he needed to say. He went 'round and 'round, hoping for a way to avoid a fight… But that wasn't going to happen.

When Eli headed toward his room, Hunter stopped him. "We're going to talk."

Eli's face was rigid. "About?"

Hunter sighed, running a hand through his hair. "Why are you so angry with Jo?"

"Why?" Eli's voice broke. "She's the reason you and mom are divorced—"

"Eli." Hunter shook his head. "That's not true."

"You're only saying that so I'll like her."

"I want you to like her, yes, but I've never lied to you. I'm not going to start now." He paused. "Your mom and I had problems that had nothing to do with Jo."

"You've made your mind up. She's who you want, no matter what I think. She's the only thing you've ever wanted."

Hunter frowned. "Son, if you weren't the most important thing in my life, I wouldn't be here, talking to you, fighting with you. But I am. I didn't run after Jo—I stayed to raise you. I thought you knew you were my world." He'd lived every single day with his son's well-being foremost in his mind. He loved his boy. Every dirty diaper, first step, scrape or tumble, call from the principal, had kept Hunter alive and breathing.

"Because she wasn't here." Eli's voice rose.

"Damn it, Eli. Whether Jo is here or she leaves, you're always my son. You'll always be first. Always."

Eli shook his head. "You said you'd never lie to me, but you are. How can I be first, if you're *with* her?"

"There are times we're not going to agree on things. I imagine it'll happen more the older you get." He paused, searching his son's face. "You don't like Jo, I get that. I won't force the two of you together anymore. Tomorrow night, the float, that's it. But in my spare time, I will see her."

"Until she leaves you again!" Eli shouted.

Hunter's nod was tight. He couldn't guarantee she'd stay, that much was true. But he'd take any time she gave him. "Until she leaves."

"Dad." Eli shook his head, seething. "You're an idiot."

"I'll tolerate you being angry, Eli. But I will not accept your disrespect. Whether you're talking to me or Miss Stephens, you will watch your tone. You hear me?"

Eli's face crumpled, his chin quivering. "Yes, *sir.*"

"It's late." His eyes stung, hot and sharp, but Hunter stood his ground. "Go on to bed now."

Eli turned, stomped down the hall and slammed the door behind him.

He didn't know what was worse, the fact that his son was hurting so much or that he had no way to make it easier. Not seeing Jo, giving her up and going back to the way it was— He couldn't do it. He loved his son, he always would. And he loved Jo, too. He'd be damned if he couldn't figure out how to have them both.

Chapter Fourteen

"Shit," Annabeth muttered. She sipped her coffee. "This is bad. Lola's probably got half the town talking about me dating this mystery man." She shook her head, then spoke up, "Cody, honey, try to chew with your mouth closed."

Cody nodded, his face covered in frosting and gingerbread crumbs.

"Why is it bad?" Josie asked. "It's not true."

Annabeth glanced at the small group of regulars who frequented the bakery each morning. "Maybe."

Josie laughed. "Maybe? So you're keeping secrets from me?"

"Pot, meet kettle," Annabeth said pointedly.

Josie glanced at Cody, who was smearing his frosting across the tabletop. "Maybe we should have this conversation later?"

Annabeth sat back, a huge smile on her face. "Um, definitely now." She saw Cody's creation. "Cody, sweetie, that's gorgeous, but please keep it on the plate for Mommy."

Cody nodded.

"He's quite the talker." Josie smiled.

Annabeth shrugged. "He's pretty quiet, but the counselor says it can be normal, after losing someone."

Josie looked at the little boy. He was precious. And fatherless.

"I just hope Miss Worley will stop the gossip before it gets carried away." Annabeth finished wiping up Cody's art with a mass of napkins. "Small towns like to talk. Which is fine as long as it's not about the elementary school principal, you know?"

Josie nodded, looking up as the little bell over the bakery door rang.

Amy stood there, her hair back in a ponytail. She wore a burgundy scrub top with the UET Vet logo on the left shoulder. She walked forward, her brown eyes fixing on Josie. "I'm here to pick up an order for the vet school." She pulled out a credit card and slapped it on the counter. "And I'm in a hurry."

Josie took the card, running it through the machine. "Was it called in?"

"Y-yes."

"Dad?" Josie called out. "Did we get an order from the vet school?"

Her father came out, carrying a large box. "Got it right here." His entire expression changed when he saw Amy, and his eyes widened as he looked at her shirt. "What—"

"I got it, Dad," Josie said, patting his arm. "Thanks."

"You sure you don't need help?" he asked.

"You have the sweetest daddy." Amy waved her fingertips at him. "Carl, you get cuter every time I see you."

He didn't say anything as he disappeared back into the kitchen.

"So, Amy." Annabeth shot Josie a look. "I didn't know you were back in town."

"For good, since Hunter got me a job at the vet school," Amy added.

Josie was very proud of the way she didn't react. She didn't burst into tears. Or scream in frustration. Or throw the box of pastries at Amy. Nope, she didn't even twitch. She stood there, staring at the credit card machine, praying it would hurry up.

"Well, isn't that something?" Annabeth pulled Cody into her lap.

"Guess the gossips haven't got wind of it yet. But when they do, tongues will be wagging." Amy laughed. "I love to give 'em something to talk about."

"And you were always so good at it." Annabeth smiled sweetly.

Amy ignored Annabeth, tapping her nails

on the counter as she asked Josie, "What's the holdup?"

"Old machine." The machine spit out the receipt, which Josie handed over. "Just needs your signature."

Amy signed it, grabbed the box, then paused. "Want me to tell Hunter hi for you when I get to work?" Her smile was a little too self-satisfied.

"Thanks but no thanks," Josie said, keeping her tone light. She could hold it together until Amy walked out. After that, all bets were off. Relief swept over her as the other woman turned to go.

But Amy turned back suddenly, her brown eyes sweeping over Josie from head to toe. "Hunter's a big boy, so it's his own fault for making the same mistakes over again. But—" she lowered her voice "—you hurt my boy, and there will be hell to pay."

Josie stared at Amy, surprised and a little impressed that the woman had any maternal instincts. She managed a tight grin. "You have a good day."

Amy left, the little bell over the bakery door breaking the silence. And just like that, the entire bakery, all eight people, were whispering and talking among themselves.

Annabeth stood, putting Cody's empty plate and cup on the counter. "Why would he get her a job?"

Josie's heart ached. "She's Eli's mom. You know Hunter. If she needs help, he's going to take care of her. For Eli." It was one of the reasons she loved Hunter. And one more reason she should book that flight straight to New Mexico. She would always have to contend with Amy, with drama, with uncertainty. Hunter might love her, but he was loyal to his family. Eli and Amy were his family. Was there really room for her?

She'd find out tonight—she had to. There was too much to sort through, too much still left unsaid. If it couldn't work, she'd start over again.

It's not as if she was tied to a place… She could go anywhere, thanks to her books.

Now she just needed to know where she was going.

"Josie?" Annabeth asked. "You okay?"

Josie nodded. "Yeah."

"You sure?"

"I think so."

The little bell rang again, and this time Lola Worley walked in.

"Is she gone?" Lola asked.

"Just missed her," Annabeth said.

Lola put her hands on her hips. "Probably for the best. I don't know what she's up to, but she had no business coming in here, stirring up trouble."

Josie shook her head. "She was picking up pastries—"

"She was stirring up trouble, mark my words," Lola affirmed. "That one lives for it. After Hunter kicked her out, she spent a good month causing fights around town, getting the men all dazed and confused by her big…" Lola waved her hands in the air. "Well, you know."

Annabeth nodded.

"Hunter kicked her out?" Josie asked.

"Teddy told me all about it. He was fit to be tied." Lola nodded. "He'd come home to find Eli in his crib, screaming and filthy. Amy was gone."

"Eli was alone?" Josie was horrified. "But—" How many times had Annabeth or her dad tried to bring up Hunter? But she'd cut them off, too caught up in herself to consider what those she'd left behind were dealing with. She hurt for Hunter. And Eli.

"He gave her a lot of chances, Josie." Annabeth nodded. "When Eli started kindergarten, he was one of those kids that was always in the office after school when it was her turn to have him. She'd forget to pick him up, or didn't want to." Annabeth looked at Lola, who nodded.

"She was real good at coming in with presents, big smiles and stories for Eli before she'd leave again." Lola moved around the counter. "That boy holds on to those memories, desperate to have a real mother, I guess."

"That's natural," Josie argued. She knew what it was like to want a mother. How many times had she made excuses for her mom? Rationalized her behavior? There were flashes of brilliance. Museum visits. Opera performances. Traveling to exotic locations... But the everyday version of her mother was something altogether different.

"Seems to me his daddy did a good enough job for two parents." Lola beamed at Cody. "Look at how big you are. I swear, you look more like your pa every time I see you, Cody."

The little boy grinned.

"You want a cookie?" Lola asked him.

"He just had one," Annabeth protested.

"One's not near enough for a growing boy." Lola winked at Cody as she handed him a huge frosting-covered sugar cookie.

Annabeth laughed. "We don't need a nap today."

Lola hugged her. "Sorry, sugar. It's the holidays, you know? Calls for extra treats and breaking the rules now and then."

Annabeth smiled. "It's fine."

Josie's father came out of the kitchen. "Did you believe that Amy? I didn't know what to say to her. Can I ban her from the shop?"

"Absolutely not." Josie sighed. "If she is back for good, we will all be on our best behavior. For Eli."

Lola, Annabeth and her father looked at her.

"Okay?" she added, needing their cooperation.

Annabeth and her dad nodded quickly.

Lola sighed and said, "I'll try, Josie, but I sure as hell won't like it."

"DR. BOONE," A VOICE called over his intercom. "Your two o'clock is here."

"Have Frank get Jester's vitals and put them in an exam room. I'll be there as soon as I can."

"Yes, Dr. Boone." And the intercom went silent.

Tripod leaped onto his desk corner.

"What are you doing here?" he asked, rubbing the black cat firmly along the back of his neck. "Too many dogs in the clinic today?"

Tripod yawned, revealing a long pink tongue.

"You go on and nap, and I'll just get back to work." Hunter gave the cat a last scratch before finalizing the chart on his tablet. The pharaoh hound was going to be a daddy. It had been a long road and the poor dog had no idea what he'd been missing out on, but puppies were definitely on the way.

"Hunter?"

Hunter looked up, completely floored to find Amy in UET scrubs. His stomach dropped. "What's with the getup?" he asked.

"I got a job." She smiled. "A tech position."

He sat back in his chair. "At the hospital?"

She nodded, coming into his office. "Yes."

"This hospital?" he clarified.

"I'll be over in the large-animal clinic, mostly." She sat in one of the chairs opposite him. "Unless someone here needs me."

"And you think this is a good idea?" he asked. "Last time we talked, you were heading to Vegas, following the circuit, living the dream."

Her smile tightened a little. "And then my son called me and asked me to come home."

Now he felt as though he'd been punched in the gut. "Eli called you?"

She sat back, looking far too comfortable in the chair. "Ask him."

"Why did he call you?"

"Hunter." She laughed the laugh that usually had any man looking at her, appreciating her. It made his skin crawl. "Contrary to what you think, some people want me around. That person just happens to be the boy we made together. He's upset."

He waited.

"Josie being here." She paused, frowning.

"Well, he's just torn up about it. He's worried about you. And about me."

"About you?" He shook his head. "You weren't here."

"But he knows I still love you." Her brown eyes bore into his. "He knows I hold out hope every single day that we'll reconcile."

"Just because I didn't go public with why we divorced then doesn't mean I'm going to keep covering it up. Eli's getting old enough to figure things out. To realize you left us long before our divorce was final." He stood, pulling on his white coat. "I don't know what you're hoping to gain, but I can't keep protecting Eli from your mistakes. This time, I won't."

She smiled up at him, shifting in her seat. "I'm not planning on making any mistakes."

"Amy, if you're on the clock, I suggest you get to work. The school doesn't run without everyone working at one hundred and ten percent. You'd be smart to remember that."

She stuck her tongue out at him. "Always so

responsible." She stood, stretching so that her chest was impossible to miss. "Fine. I'll see you later on. I was thinking of having Eli for a sleepover tonight."

"We'll talk later." He brushed by her, heading straight to the clinic.

This was the last thing he needed. Eli was already stretched too thin. Throw his mom back in the mix, let her play her victim card and things would get bad.

"They're in exam four," Martha said once he'd reached the admissions desk.

He nodded, opening the door to find Jester. The dog growled, deep in his throat, a nerve-racking sound considering Jester was a nasty-tempered mix that tipped the scales at almost two hundred pounds.

"How's he doing?" Hunter asked Clarence Shaw, Jester's owner.

"He walked into the door frame today." Clarence shrugged. "I can't stand to see him this way, Doc. You gotta fix him up."

Hunter scanned the dog's chart. "You sure?"

Clarence patted the broad head of the massive dog. "He's my baby, Doc. I'm sure. How long until he's better?"

"Cataracts are pretty bad." Hunter kept his voice steady, soothing for Jester—and Clarence. "Especially for a dog this age. After the surgery, he'll be seeing in a few hours."

"No kidding?"

"No kidding." Hunter stood, rubbing the dog's head and neck.

"He'll like that." Clarence was smiling. "Hell, I'll like that. It's hard on a body, carryin' Jester around."

Hunter smiled. "I can imagine."

Jester lay flat, resting his head on his paws. "You'll be fine, big fella. You'll see," Hunter said.

"What's next?" Clarence asked.

It took twenty minutes to get Jester checked in to the hospital and settled in a cage.

Tripod came around the corner as Hunter

closed the cage door. "I'd stay away from this one, Tripod. He can't see you." He watched the three-legged cat wind his way between his legs. "Either way, I imagine he'd rather eat you than cuddle with you."

"Dr. Boone." Mario, a tech, laughed. "I'll keep Tripod out of Jester's way."

Hunter grinned. "I'll check in on him tomorrow."

"Headed to the parade?" Mario asked. "Tell Eli good luck with the float."

"I will." He nodded his goodbyes, heading back to his office. He hung his coat on the rack and dug for his keys. With a quick glance around the room, he flipped off the light and locked the door behind him.

"Dr. Boone." Dr. Lee was in the hallway. "I was wondering if you'd heard anything from Miss Stephens. Any interest in the mural project?"

"I'm on my way to see her now." He tugged on his jacket. "I'll see what she's thinking."

"I'd appreciate that." Dr. Lee smiled. "Enjoy your evening."

"You, too." He nodded.

"Thank you for sending Mrs. Boone to us. It seems you have a very talented family."

Hunter stopped cold. "I didn't send Amy to you, Dr. Lee. To be perfectly candid, I would not have recommended her."

"Oh, I see." Dr. Lee frowned. "I suppose we'll have to make the best of it. Enjoy your evening."

The drive from the hospital to the bakery took fifteen minutes. It took every second of that time to ease the tension from his shoulders. He wanted to enjoy tonight, enjoy being with Jo. The streets were blocked for the night's celebration, so he had to walk, which did him good. Nothing like seeing the smiling faces of the community, the kids piled in the backs of minivans or sitting in lawn chairs to set things right again.

By the time he reached Pop's Bakery, he wasn't

thinking about Amy or Dr. Lee or the pile of charts he needed to review.

He pushed into the bakery, the little bell chiming. Most of the lights were off, but he heard movement in the back room.

"Jo?" he called out. Sprinkles greeted him by jumping up and down and yapping excitedly. "Good to see you, too—especially since you're not throwing up or needing a diaper."

He walked through the connecting door from the bakery to Carl's house. "Jo?"

"Hunter?" she called out, her voice thin and stressed.

He followed the sound of her voice to her bedroom.

She was sitting on the bed, bundled in her robe, tear tracks down her face. She rubbed her nose with the back of her hand and sniffed, loudly. He didn't know whether to laugh or pull her into his lap. He sat and drew her close. "What's wrong Jo?"

She shook her head, hiccuping. "N-nothing."

"Come on now. Something's wrong. You're not one to cry for nothing."

Her big eyes peered up at him. "You mean I wasn't… For all you know I c-cry at the drop of a hat."

"Okay." He wiped the tears from her cheeks. "I'd still like to know why you're crying."

"My dad—" She sniffed. "My dad proposed to Lola."

"And that's bad?" He wasn't sure how to respond.

"No. It's g-great." She sobbed.

He laughed again.

"It's not f-funny," she moaned, pressing her face against his chest.

"Sorry." He cleared his throat. "It's not funny. And it's not bad. But you're crying."

She nodded.

His hold tightened on her. "What can I do, Jo?"

He felt her breathe deep, felt her hands grip his shirtfront. "I'm happy for him. And relieved. H-he doesn't need me to stay."

Her words clawed at his heart. "You think so?"

"I want him to be happy. And Lola is wonderful. She'll keep him young—" Her voice broke. Her hands twisted in the flannel of his shirt.

"He wants you to stay, Jo." The words rasped out.

She froze, looking up at him. Her silver-gray eyes were full of pain, bone-crushing misery. "I'm a h-horrible daughter."

He laughed then, though he tried not to. "You are not."

"I am, Hunter." She swallowed, her gaze wandering over his face. "A good daughter wouldn't be jealous."

His hand cupped her face. "Jealous?"

"I hate that I'm the way…I am." She frowned.

"What way?" He frowned, too. "I don't understand."

"I'm t-terrified."

"Of what?"

"Commitments and relationships, losing control." She sighed, sniffing. "Hurting others to get what I want. Like you. And Eli." Her gaze wandered to his mouth. "You make me remember how to feel things I've tried to forget. And it scares me."

He rubbed his nose against hers. Her words revealed so much. "Let me love you, Jo."

He felt her tremble and pulled her close. His lips were firm, parting hers and stealing her breath. She shuddered again, but he didn't let her go. He didn't care if they were late for the festivities. Right now, he was where he needed to be.

Chapter Fifteen

Josie rested her head on Hunter's chest, listening to the thump of his racing heart. Her hand drifted back and forth across his bare chest and stomach, stroking the muscles along his side. He offered comfort and strength, surrounding her with his warmth. She closed her eyes, tempted to stay put. She didn't really want to ride on the float, anyway. But they were already late. Any later and people might come looking for them.

She sat up, running a hand over her tangle of curls. "We should go."

"Like this? Lola will have plenty to talk about."

She giggled. "Um, no. Clothes, taming this—" she pointed to her hair "—and *then* we go."

He lay there, naked and gorgeous. "You okay?"

She nodded, enjoying the view a little too much. "Sorry."

He sat up, smoothing her hair from her face. "For?"

"Crying. Being pathetic." She shrugged. "Being emotionally overwrought. It was a long day."

He nodded. "I hear ya."

She attempted to pull her robe from beneath him. Since he wouldn't give it up, she stood, bravely walking across the room to pull clothes from her closet. "Anything new at the hospital?"

"A dog. A monster of a dog." He chuckled. "Two hundred pounds of drool and muscle."

She pulled her panties up and looked at him. "Two hundred pounds?" She arched an eyebrow. "Are you telling me a fish story?"

He shook his head. "Nope. You should go like that." He nodded at her pink-and-white cotton undies.

She pulled on her red bra, clasped it in front and saw his frown. "Hunter." She laughed. "So what does this beast need you to do to fix him, Dr. Boone?"

"He can't see."

"Poor baby." She frowned. "What's the matter with him? I mean, can you fix him?"

"Yep. The hospital can handle almost anything. He's got some terrible cataracts, but he'll be fine." He pulled his pants on, giving her the most delightful glimpse of his firm rear and muscled thighs. "Speaking of the hospital…"

That doused the rising hunger. She gripped her red sweater, waiting. "Yes?"

"Dr. Lee wanted me to touch base with you about the mural." He pulled on his undershirt, then started buttoning up his plaid flannel shirt. "You said you wanted to at dinner, but I didn't want to speak for you."

She'd thought about it a lot. Working with Hunter was a perk. Doing something for this family, honoring their son, was important. Supporting the school, also significant. She'd made up her mind to do it. But Amy changed everything. "I don't think I can work there." And since he wasn't going to bring it up, she would. "Not with Amy around." She pulled her brown corduroy pants on and looked at him. "She came by the bakery this morning—"

"I'm sure she did."

"She had an order to pick up for the hospital." She ran her fingers through her hair, distracted.

"She's not happy unless she's making everyone else unhappy." There was no mistaking his frustration. "Not the best way to start the day, I imagine." He brushed her hair from her shoulders, tilting her head back so they were eye to eye.

"She said you got her the job," Josie whispered.

His eyes narrowed, his brow furrowing deeply. When she slipped from his hold, he didn't stop her. But she noticed the way his jaw muscle ticked as she met his gaze in the mirror. "You think I got her the job?" he asked.

She picked up a clip, fiddling with the clasp.

"It made sense. She's family. You help your family out—"

"I found out she was working there today." He came up behind her, slipping his arms around her waist and pulling her against his chest. He spoke clearly, leaving no room for interpretation, "I didn't help her get the job, Jo. And while it's generous of you to think I'd be that self-sacrificing, I'm not. I might help her get a job, in Houston or Amarillo. But not here, not now."

"Oh." She couldn't stop the smile from spreading across her face.

"Oh?" He laughed, spinning her around and pulling her against him. His face grew earnest and real and so damn gorgeous her heart was on the verge of bursting from her chest. His kiss was featherlight, but his words made her lightheaded. "I love you, Jo. I'm doing my best not to screw things up here."

She blinked. He said it. He loved her.

"Come on." He glanced at his watch. "We're

late. Any later and people *will* talk." His kiss was deep, leaving her heart and body spinning.

"Because we're late?" she asked, still processing.

He smiled, stroking his fingertips over her cheek. "You don't know what you want yet—I get that." His voice faltered. "Until you do, I'd rather keep things a little discreet." He kissed her forehead, sighing. "That way it'll be easier for Eli, your dad and me if you go. We'll still be here, you know?"

He wasn't embarrassed or ashamed—he was protecting her, protecting her father and his son. And she loved him all the more for it. She should tell him. She should say it. But a flash of Eli, of Amy's smug grin and the agony of losing Hunter silenced her.

"I need five minutes," she pleaded, pointing to the makeup.

"You don't need it." He shook his head but gave her enough time to put on some mascara, a little eye shadow and some bright red holiday-cheer lipstick.

"Ready?" He took her in, head to toe, before shaking his head. "I'm fine being late, Jo." He pulled her close, bending forward to kiss her.

She laughed, covering his lips with her fingers. "I'm ready."

He pressed a kiss to her fingers, sighing dramatically. "Fine."

She shook her head but took the hand he offered her. "How's Mars?" she asked as they put on their coats and headed out of the bakery.

"She's good, taking a few steps. Her pups are a handful, so we're not letting them nurse all the time. Their poor mama needs time to recover." He paused. "Owners offered me a pup and I'm thinking about giving one to my dad." Hunter led her around the corner.

"Wow," she said finally, looking at all the floats, the lights, the carolers, the canopies that dotted the courthouse lawn. The air hummed with excitement, warding off some of the night chill. "Was it this big when we were in high school?"

"Gets bigger every year. Good to see you, Lance." Hunter nodded at someone but kept them moving.

She called out "hellos" and "nice to see yous" as Hunter led them around another corner. Their float was waiting, hooked up to a large hunter green truck with *Boone Ranch and Rehabilitation Reserve* on the doors. The younger kids were all giggling and playing tag while the older kids were checking the garland and float decorations.

"They're here," someone called out. All the kids waved.

Hunter waved back, giving her a quick grin over his shoulder.

"They wanted to send out a search party," Fisher whispered to Hunter as they walked up. "I figured that might not be the best idea. Didn't want them to find you two in a compromising situation. Might scar them for life."

Hunter punched him in the shoulder. "Got sidetracked with—"

Fisher held up his hands. "Don't need or want to know."

Josie couldn't help but notice Eli. The boy looked so downtrodden, she wanted to hug him. But since she was probably the reason he was upset, she should keep her hugs to herself. His one long, lingering glance at Dara spoke volumes, though.

"Hey, Miss Josie." Dara was red-cheeked and excited, her green sparkly Santa hat and mittens only adding to her adorableness. "Your chair is nice and secure. I rode on it here, just to make sure."

"Thanks, Dara." Josie hugged the girl, surveying the float. It looked even better now, the fairy-light glow illuminating the hours of work the kids had put into making *34* and *Floppy Feet* come to life. "It's just amazing. You guys did a really incredible job." She spoke to Eli, too, who was circling the perimeter of the trailer to check that the garlands and lights were secure.

Eli looked at her, then Dara, shoved his hands in his pockets and mumbled, "Guess so." His attention wandered back to Dara, but the girl was making a point of ignoring him.

Josie didn't know what to say, or do. Young love could seriously suck.

"Are you Joselyn Stephens?" A man approached, his smile a little too appreciative.

She didn't recognize him. "Yes."

"Renata Boone suggested I interview you for the piece we're putting together on the best undiscovered small towns of Texas." He held his hand out. "Ray Garza, State Tourism Department."

"Nice to meet you." Josie shook his hand.

"Would you be free after the parade? We'll be set up by the stage to get some shots for the special." His smile grew. "I'll find you a cup of hot chocolate and let you show me around."

Josie glanced at Hunter, who was watching

with interest. "Renata would be better suited for showing you around, Mr. Garza."

"Call me Ray." His smile might be charming, but the way he looked her up and down made her skin crawl.

"Ray." She didn't smile in return. "I'm not sure there's much I can say to sell Stonewall Crossing. It sort of speaks for itself."

"I'd like to hear a little more about what you mean by that." There it was again, that sweeping, slightly-too-lascivious-to-be-ignored appraisal of her figure. He was far too interested in her chest. "We'll meet you by the stage, with hot chocolate, after the parade, then."

Hunter took her hand in his. "You ready, Miss Celebrity?" He shot Ray Garza a look—a look that spoke volumes. She loved that look.

"I guess so." She took his hand and stepped up onto the float. "I'm happy to chat with you for a bit right after the parade, Mr. Garza."

Ray Garza shook his head. "I won't take up much time, I promise. Tonight's about spending time with family." Ray Garza nodded at Hunter, then her, and headed to the small stage where the parade judges were seated, smack-dab in the middle of the square.

"You need an escort for that interview?" Hunter asked, watching Ray Garza go.

She chuckled, leaning over the side of the trailer. "Jealous, Dr. Boone? Don't you know I prefer my men in white coats?"

Hunter looked up at her, tipping his hat back. "I recall hearing something along those lines."

If he kept smiling at her like that, she'd kiss him—no matter who was watching.

He winked at her and stepped back, helping the younger kids climb aboard. She watched his every move, the way he swung each kid high, giving them a word or smile of encouragement. He knew them all, cared about them, about this. This was his home, a place as ingrained in his blood as the color of his incredible eyes.

She'd never felt that way about a place. But something about the camaraderie and affection among this bunch made her rethink, again, the value in her solitary life.

Hunter's voice was stern as he called out, "Remember the rules." He paused, making certain all eyes were on him before he continued. "No standing up, no moving around and no horseplay. Your job is to stay safe, sit on your hay bale and wave like crazy at all the people. And don't forget to yell out 'Merry Christmas' now and then. Got it?"

A dozen hat-and-scarf-clad heads nodded. There was something poignant about their red noses, bright eyes and on-the-verge-of-bursting-with-excitement energy. The mood was contagious. Josie sat in the chair, tucking her hands under her legs. It was cold and, in their haste, she'd forgotten her gloves.

"Miss Stephens?" The little girl had red braids peeking out from under her hat and a smattering of freckles across her nose. "Are you really going to read to us? *Floppy Feet* is my favorite.

I have two rabbits that look just like the ones in your book."

"You do?" Josie asked, a sudden warmth chasing away the cold. "What are their names?"

"Floppy and Jack," the little girl answered.

Josie laughed. "Those are great names." She took the book Eli thrust in her face. It was old, the paper jacket creased and worn. There was a faint ring on the back cover, where someone had probably put their iced tea or coffee cup. "Thanks, Eli." She glanced at the boy, wishing he'd give some sort of acknowledgment that she existed. She wanted to ask if this was his copy, the one Hunter and Fisher had read to him when he was little. But the words got stuck in her throat.

He looked at her then, searching her face for one long moment. He swallowed so hard she knew he was holding something back.

"Thank you," Josie repeated, feeling the all-too-familiar sting in her eyes.

"Come on, Eli." Hunter waved his son to the

side of the trailer. "Your job is to keep an eye on the little ones," he said to Eli, Dara and four older teenagers who were helping corral the youngsters. Hunter shot her one more smile before climbing into the truck cab.

When the truck pulled forward, the kids squealed with glee. Josie beamed, glancing around the trailer at each little face. The teenagers were smiling, too. Even Eli. Until he saw her smiling at him.

HUNTER NODDED AT the thumbs-up in his side mirror from Eli. Some garland had fallen loose as they cleared the last stretch of road, but everything was secure again.

"Can you go any slower?" Fisher asked as they scooted an inch forward.

"Got a hot date I don't know about?" Hunter glanced at his brother.

"No. But we might just get the kids back to their folks before midnight," his brother shot back.

"I guess a little thing like the twenty kids on the flatbed trailer we're pulling shouldn't matter?" Hunter glanced at the clock on his dashboard. "For the record, it's nine-fifteen."

Fisher snorted. "Look who's all feisty tonight."

Hunter grinned.

The parade had gone well. No one had fallen out or pitched a fit. The lights and music had stayed on. And, from what he could tell, everyone had enjoyed their turn around the square.

As he pulled the truck and trailer into the large parking lot behind the senior center, he saw the sea of parents and cars waiting for their kids. He edged forward slowly, making sure they weren't hanging out onto the street, and parked.

He was cordial to the waiting parents, smiling and shaking hands and enjoying the overall success of the evening. But inside, he felt like a teenager again. A teenager who wanted, more than anything, to get Jo, take her hand in his and savor the rest of the night together.

He caught a look at her, all red-cheeked and

wild curls. She was still sitting in her chair, a little girl on her lap. The two of them were reading *Floppy Feet*, so engrossed in the story that neither seemed aware of what was happening around them.

"Kelsey," the little girl's mother finally said. "I imagine Miss Stephens is ready to get out of this cold."

"Aw, Momma." Kelsey frowned.

"I'll read the book to you tonight," her mother coerced.

Kelsey wriggled from Jo's lap, shooting Jo one big gap-toothed grin before running over to Hunter. "Thanks for letting me ride."

"Hope you had fun."

She nodded, wrapping her arms around her mother's neck.

He looked at Jo, the yearning on her face as she watched Kelsey and her mother startling him. She caught him staring and rolled her eyes. Damn, but she was beautiful.

"What can I do?" she asked, nodding at Eli,

Dara and Tyler. They were already uncoiling the lights and garlands, making neat coils and stacking them aside.

"They'll get most of it. So nothing flies off on the way back to the ranch." He waved at the older teens working. "You can keep an eye on the two strays," he teased, nodding at two little boys hopping from hale bale to hay bale around the trailer's edge.

He turned to Jo. "Once they're back with their herd, I'll get you to your interview." If she left, tonight would be one of those memories that he held on to for years to come. It wasn't just the sex, though sex with Jo was truly special—it was the intimacy they shared, the connection. He'd be damned if he let her go without a fight.

"What's that look for?" she asked, her pale eyes studying him.

He shook his head, knowing this wasn't the time or place to make his case. "I'll tell you later."

"Dr. Boone, this is hardly the time or place for your wayward thoughts."

"Wayward thoughts?" He bent forward. "What did *you* think I was thinking about?"

She blushed, swallowing.

Every inch of him hardened. "You can tell me about it later." His whisper was rough.

"Dad," Eli called out. "This tire looks low."

It tore his heart out to see the smile Jo gave his son. Eli didn't smile back but, for the first time, he didn't glare at her, either. For Hunter, it was progress. Jo clearly didn't see it that way.

"Duty calls." He excused himself. Eli was right. They'd have to air up the tire before they made the drive back to the ranch. "Good catch," he said, ruffling his son's hair.

Eli groaned, but Dara's soft laugh turned Eli's frown into a grin.

Hunter glanced back and forth between his son and Dara. She'd gone back to working on the trailer while Eli stood staring at her. Hunter nudged him, gently, before heading back to Jo, the boys and their newly arrived parents.

He was shaking hands with the boys' fathers when Amy arrived. He barely managed to keep his face neutral. Last thing he needed to do was make things worse with Eli. His son was barely speaking to him as it was.

"That was adorable, ya'll," Amy cooed. "Eli, honey, I think it's the best float yet."

"Thanks, Mom," Eli murmured. Hunter watched him blush as Amy draped an arm around his shoulders. "I didn't do it on my own." Eli glanced around. He might not be as grown-up as the others, but he hated being treated like a child. Especially in public.

"I know." Amy's brown eyes paused on him for a split second before she turned to Jo. Hunter braced himself as Amy said, "You must be tick-led pink to have a whole float dedicated to you, Josie." She paused. "I mean, your books."

Hunter fought to keep his reactions in check. Amy was a master at manipulation, charming and soft-spoken one minute, ripping out the jugular the next. Not that Amy would ever let that side of her show—not with her son at her side. She needed him to think the best of her. It was one of the only things that assured she'd behave in public.

Jo looked lost, her gaze bouncing between Amy, Eli and himself. "It's amazing," she finally said. "These kids are—"

"Amazing?" Amy's teasing was infused with a healthy dose of sarcasm, sarcasm neither he nor Jo missed.

Jo nodded, not taking the bait.

He held out his hand, helping Jo from the trailer. When her feet were on the ground, she pulled her hand from his, barely meeting his eyes. "I think I'll go meet with Mr. Garza now." Her voice was thin, tentative.

He nodded even though he wanted to grab her hand and keep her at his side. "I'll catch up to you in a bit," he offered, wishing he could say more. Instead, he watched her walk back to the main square, her hands stuffed deep in her coat pockets.

"Sounds like you've got plans." Amy looked at him, eyes narrowed. "So I guess I can steal our son?" She turned to Eli. "You done for the night?"

"I guess." Eli shrugged. "I was gonna hang around for a while."

Hunter didn't miss his son's quick glance at Dara. But Amy was oblivious.

"You can hang out with them anytime." Amy tucked her arm through Eli's. "How long has it been since we had a sleepover, anyway?"

"Where?" Hunter asked, leaden concern filling his belly.

"My hotel." Amy smiled. "I haven't found a real place to rent…yet. I'm staying at the Main Street Hotel. And there's two beds and cable," she added. "We can get a pizza or something, whatever you want."

Hunter watched Eli's every reaction. His son was uncertain, which Hunter understood. He had a tough choice to make. He could keep Eli from spending the night with Amy, but then he'd ensure Amy was the victim and Eli her defender.

His son looked at him, bracing for a fight.

Hunter didn't fist his hands or clench his jaw or bite out, "Your call," no matter how much he wanted to. Instead, he managed to keep it together, staying neutral and calm.

Which didn't sit well with Eli. "Thanks, Mom. If you're sure you don't have any plans. Wouldn't want to get in the way." Eli shoved his hands in his pockets, staring at the ground at his feet.

"Eli." Hunter's voice was low. "You're never in the way, ever."

Amy glared at Hunter, the look on her face a visible replay of the argument they'd had on his porch the week before.

"Yeah, sure." Eli's tone sharpened, and he outright scowled as he added, "You have fun tonight."

Hunter could tell Eli to get his butt in the truck—his every instinct told him to do just that.

He could drive his son home and the two of them could have another fight over Jo and Amy. But then he'd end up with a son who hated him, an all but sainted ex-wife, no Jo and no closer to resolution on any account. And, no matter how impossible it seemed right this second, he wanted the best possible outcome for everyone.

He took a deep breath. "I don't appreciate your tone. And we've talked about this. You're never in the way." He shook his head, searching for the right words. "I understand wanting to spend time with your mom. If that's what you want to do tonight, then go ahead. But don't think you have to go or that I want you to go, all right?"

Eli's anger faltered, his blue-green eyes going wide.

"You're going on a date with someone he can't stand." Amy's words were quick, tipping the scales in resentment's favor. "Of course he doesn't want to stay. How do you expect him to feel, Hunter?"

There wasn't anything he could say to that, not

without making things ten times worse. He hated that Amy put words in Eli's mouth, that she had no problem using Eli to vent her thoughts and opinions. But Eli was old enough to speak up now. How many times had his son challenged him? Until Eli set Amy straight, Hunter's hands were tied. He watched Amy leading him toward her truck. "You want to get something to eat first? Some hot chocolate or something?"

Hunter stood waiting, hoping for some sort of look or acknowledgment, some sort of softening in his son. But Eli never looked back. Hunter watched Amy's taillights disappear.

"You okay, Dr. Boone?" Dara asked.

Hunter nodded, working hard at a smile. "I'll give ya'll a hand." He set to work beside the others, getting the trailer ready for the drive back to the ranch.

Chapter Sixteen

The phone was ringing. Josie glanced at the clock. It was three in the morning.

Who would call at this hour? Her mom? Lola?

She sat up, pulled on her robe and ran to the phone. Not that her dad would hear it, since he took his hearing aids out at night.

"Hello?" She was a little breathless and barely awake, so it came out like a croak.

"Josie? Miss Stephens?" The voice was high, strained and scared. "It's Eli. Eli Boone."

"Eli?" Josie came fully awake in seconds. An ice-cold weight ballooned in her stomach. "Is everything okay?"

"I guess…" There was a tremor in his voice. He was scared. "Didn't know who else to call."

"It's fine." She prompted, really worried now. "You can call anytime."

"Yeah…" Eli's voice broke. "Can you come get me?"

Something was very wrong. Her fingers tangled in the phone cord as she processed his words. "Where are you?" She spoke as calmly as possible.

"My mom's hotel room. Roadside Motel, next to the gas station and the bar."

"Off the highway?" she asked, knowing which place he was talking about and hoping Eli was wrong. She had a hard time believing Hunter would approve. To hear Lola talk about it, if something shady or illegal was happening, it had to have started at *that* bar. Of course, Lola was known for dramatics… Still, the bar was in the middle of the hotel parking lot where Eli was. "Where's your mom?"

"Don't know. Woke up and she was gone. She's not answering her cell phone."

"Did you call your dad—"

"I called Uncle Fisher and Uncle Ryder, but they didn't answer. Dad's working. And he'd get really mad and they'd fight and I...I just want to go home." He cleared his throat. "Will you come get me, please?"

Josie's heart was in her throat. "I'll be there in five minutes." There was no way she could refuse him.

"Thanks," he murmured, then hung up.

She tugged on her father's boots, pulled her black wool coat over her blue plaid flannel pajamas, grabbed her rental car keys and headed out the door. It was eerily quiet up and down Main Street. Most of Stonewall Crossing was asleep, the storefronts darkened and the streets deserted. She drove on, reaching the edge of Main Street as it intersected the highway. The Roadside Motel was there, off the on-ramp, next door to a run-down bar and a twenty-four-hour truck stop. She might not have any kids, but this was not the sort of place you left a child alone.

She pulled into the parking lot, focused on the windows of the motel for any sign of Eli. She slammed on her brakes as room seven's curtains dropped and the door opened. Eli all but ran out, a duffel bag over his shoulder and his cowboy hat on his head.

He nodded at her as he climbed into the car.

"You okay?" she asked.

He nodded again.

"Did you leave your mom a note?" Josie asked. "So she doesn't get back and worry over you?"

Eli snorted then.

"She will, Eli."

"I left a note," he grumbled, hugging his duffel bag close.

"Okay, good. Want me to take you home?"

He looked at her. "Yeah."

"You're shivering," she said, turning up the heat as he snapped his seat belt into place.

"Heater in the room was broken." He shrugged, holding his hands out to the warm air.

She looked at him, fighting back a million questions. Rage wasn't an emotion she was familiar with. But right now, she was so furious with Amy she could barely see straight.

Eli looked at her.

Amy and anger could wait. She searched his face. He was so mature for his age, but she knew he had to be hurting right now. "We should call your dad," she murmured.

"He'll get all riled up." Eli frowned. "You don't understand."

And while Josie thought Hunter had every right to get upset over his son being left in some off-the-highway one-night-stand motel, she suspected Eli wouldn't want to hear that. "You'll talk to him as soon as you get home?"

He nodded.

She didn't want to be in the middle of anything. She didn't want to keep secrets from

Hunter, not where Eli was concerned. "Thank you." She beamed at the boy.

He was watching her closely. "Dad said your mom wasn't the best in the world."

She answered carefully, trying to decide what she should or shouldn't say. "That's true." She added, "She loved me. I know she did the best she could by me." Josie put the car in Drive, turning them in the opposite direction. "She didn't really know what to do with me."

"What do you mean?"

She hesitated for a minute. "My mom wasn't the motherly type. She was more interested in her…hobbies." Men, marriage, weddings, that sort of thing.

"Guess my mom and your mom have a lot in common." His words were soft, but sad.

Even though she wasn't her mother's biggest fan, it was a hard comparison to hear. "You think so?" she asked, offering Eli the chance to vent. Whatever had happened between Amy and her son, he'd needed rescuing tonight. And he'd called her to do the rescuing.

"Rodeo calls and, bam, Mom's there. *I* call?" He shook his head, anger coloring his words. "She doesn't show up when she says she will. But when she does, she's full of…of *it*." His hold on his bag tightened. "She believes what she says when she says it, but it never lasts. Like tonight, telling me and Dad we were staying in town, ordering pizza and hanging out." He sucked in a deep breath, calming a little before he went on. "Dad always tells me to be careful—to not get my hopes up. And that really bugs me, because I hate that he's right about her. If he'd just believe in her, she might change, you know?"

She knew exactly what he wanted to hear. "Nice thought, that someone can change someone else. I wish it was true."

"It might help."

"It might." She retreated a little, desperate to keep him talking. "But my experience is change is a personal choice, Eli."

"I guess… She's my mom, you know?"

"I do." And she did. She really did. She smiled at the boy again.

"Dad doesn't get it. His mom was the best."

"She was," Josie agreed, remembering Mags Boone with real affection. "She was pretty much the perfect wife and mother. She kept a neat house, always had food on hand for anyone who stopped by, and looked put together without trying." Josie laughed. "Of course, I was used to my mother, so Mags was like a real-live fairy godmother. She liked everyone—"

"She didn't like my mom," Eli interrupted.

Josie could imagine that. Mags had always been fiercely protective of her boys. Sure, Amy hadn't gotten pregnant on her own, but Mags would have found a way to believe it wasn't Hunter's fault. It was the first time Josie ever felt even the slightest twinge of sympathy for Amy. One glance at the ten-year-old boy and the sympathy was gone.

"I don't think they ever made Mom feel welcome," Eli muttered. "Maybe that's why she leaves. Maybe she comes back, thinking things will be different. Then she sees it's still the same and there's not enough here to stick around for."

She looked at Eli and ached. *You are enough.* She blinked back tears. *He* was enough. Amy had this amazing boy's love and she chose to leave. She sniffed, tears dangerously close to spilling over. If he was hers, he'd have been her world and she'd make sure he knew it.

Eli continued, "Guess I feel like I need to make up for that."

"Oh, Eli, that's a big job for one man."

He nodded. "Guess so."

"All you can do is love her," Josie said. She glanced at Eli, who was staring out the front windshield, jaw clenched and hands fisted in the straps of his duffel bag. Life could be hard. But for someone like Eli, with a family who would move heaven and earth for him, it didn't need to be. She tried again. "We have something else in common, Eli."

"What?" He glanced at her.

"Our fathers are amazing. My dad would bend over backward to help me out. He's always there, full of advice." She paused, shooting him a conspiratorial look. "Even when I don't want him to be."

Eli nodded, his short laugh a relief.

"He's the person I call when my world is falling apart. Or when I have news I have to share with someone because I'm bursting with excitement, ya know?" She glanced at him.

"Yeah." His answer was soft.

"I am sorry about tonight, Eli." She turned onto the road leading into the Boone ranch. "I wish I could make it better."

There was silence before he asked, "You do?"

She swallowed. "I do. I really do." She slowed down as a rabbit sprinted across the road and into the opposite field.

"You can drop me here," Eli said, pointing at the Lodge. "Dad's working emergency duty."

"I know you're worried about your dad being

mad. But if he is mad, it's because he loves you so much." She kept the car and the heater running. "Talk to him, Eli, okay?"

"I will. I gotta sort out what I'm going to say." Eli nodded, gathering his things.

"That makes sense," she agreed.

"Thanks for the ride." He looked at her, a shadow of a smile on his face.

She watched him climb the steps of the Lodge, waiting until he was safely inside before turning around and heading back into town. Thoughts of Eli and Hunter and Amy went 'round and 'round. Should she call Hunter? She didn't know if she'd done the right thing. Eli had called and she'd responded. Maybe she'd overstepped, but surely Hunter would understand.

By the time she parked her car at the bakery, her head ached. She slumped over the steering wheel, second-guessing every minute since Eli's phone call.

The bakery lights flipped on, startling Josie. She glanced at the clock on the car dashboard.

Five o'clock. Dad would be up, making coffee, letting the dog out and getting things ready for the morning. She watched as Lola and her father appeared, smiling and talking, carrying mugs of coffee. It was a glimpse of her father's future and she liked what she saw.

Now, if only she had a crystal ball to see what her future looked like.

HUNTER DIDN'T SEE Amy's truck in the parking lot. Where were they? He'd texted her he was on his way. He yawned, wiping the sleep from his eyes. He'd been called in to scope a Great Dane who'd managed to swallow his tennis ball on a rope. After a two-hour surgery, the ball and rope were removed from the dog's stomach and intestine. One thing he could say about his job, it was never boring. He still found real satisfaction working with animals, even when he got next to no sleep.

Once he picked up Eli, he'd go see Jo at Pop's,

get some kolaches and go home for a few hours of sleep.

He knew Jo's time clock was ticking. He knew she loved New Mexico, and the job she'd been offered was right up her alley. But she needed to know that he wanted her to stay, with him, here. And he was going to make sure he said that, no misunderstandings or miscommunications.

He stepped out of his truck at the same time Amy's truck plowed into the Main Street Hotel's lot. Her vehicle bounced as she came to a complete stop, then her door flew open and she charged at him.

"What the hell is the matter with you?" she yelled.

He sighed, crossing his arms over his chest. He was too tired for her drama this morning. "Morning to you, too."

She poked his chest with her finger. "Morning? Are you shittin' me?"

"Where's Eli?"

Amy paused, took a step back. "What do you mean?"

He waited.

"She came and picked him up this morning," Amy snapped.

"Who came and picked him up?"

"Josie." She frowned. "You didn't send her to get him? She said you did. She said you called her to come get him."

He was beyond confused now. Why would Jo pick up Eli? Why would she tell Amy he'd sent her? Why would Eli go with Jo? He wasn't exactly her biggest fan. "Where is he?"

"I don't know." Her voice spiked. "She has him. Why did she take him? Why did she lie?"

Hunter watched Amy. Something wasn't adding up. For one thing, Jo wasn't the one with the track record for lying. "When did she get him?"

"Must have been around seven—"

"Where were you?" he cut in, frustration giving way to anger.

"*I* was in the shower." She shook her head.

"She comes and takes our son who knows where and lies about it and you want to know where I was? Damn, Hunter, are you that blind to that woman?"

Hunter sighed. "I'll call Eli."

"Already tried," she argued. "His phone is off, I guess."

His eyes narrowed. "I will talk to him—"

"Good. Go talk to him. Now. After you find him." She shook her head, climbing into her truck. "I'm not gonna argue with you when I could be looking for my son. I've half a mind to press charges against her."

Hunter watched her peel out of the parking lot as he climbed into his truck. Even though he was pretty sure Eli was with Jo, there was no fighting the fear in his heart until he knew for sure. He picked up his phone, headed toward home and called his father. Eli was most likely there. Those two were peas in a pod.

"Figured you'd call." His father answered on the first ring.

"He there?"

"Sleeping."

Hunter rubbed a hand over his face, relief so sharp he was almost breathless. "You couldn't call?" He tried not to snap.

"Whoa now, boy," his father soothed. "I called the hospital. You were in surgery."

Hunter sighed. "Thanks, Dad. Sorry. Amy—"

"I can imagine." He paused. "She with you?"

"No, but I should probably let her know where Eli is. Be there soon." He hung up and called Amy.

"What?" she snapped.

"He's at my dad's."

"Oh, thank God." Her voice was muffled. "Hunter found him." She was louder then, her voice unsteady. "Is he okay?"

"He's asleep. I'm on my way."

"I'm coming—"

"No." He was going to talk to his son alone.

"No?" She was crying then. "No? My son gets taken from my hotel room, disappears, and now you're not going to let me see him?" Her voice was muffled again. "No, Officer, I don't know about pressing charges yet."

Hunter groaned. "I'll call you later." Ten minutes later he was inside the Lodge, staring down at his bleary-eyed son.

Eli started with "I'm sorry."

"For what?" He sat on the bed by his son. "First thing I need to know. You okay?" When Eli started crying, Hunter pulled him into his arms and held him close. Sometimes he forgot how young Eli was. Sometimes he forgot how sweet his hair smelled, how small his frame felt against him, but he never forgot how much he loved his son.

"Yeah." His answer was muffled against Hunter's neck.

"You sure?" he asked, holding his son tighter.

"I should have called you," he said. "She...she said you wanted me to come to Granddad's, so I went with her."

He froze. "She?" He tried to pull Eli back, to look at him, but his son was clinging to him.

"Josie…" Eli cleared his throat. "She said you were working and she was going to take me home."

Jo? It didn't make sense. Jo didn't want anything to do with Amy—she'd done her best to avoid all interaction with his ex-wife. Stirring up trouble like this, out of the blue, didn't add up.

Eli was sobbing and Eli didn't cry. Even when he was a toddler, he'd rarely had tantrums. Whatever had happened, his son was torn up about it. "What's got you so worked up?"

"I didn't want you to be mad at me."

"Worried is more like it."

"And M-Mom's phone message. She was s-so worried." He sniffed. "I didn't mean to worry her like that. You can't blame her or be mad at her or not let me see her anymore. It's not her fault."

Hunter sighed, hearing Amy's words. "Eli, what happened?"

Eli sat back, frowning. "I told you."

"Nothing else? You didn't talk to Jo when she was driving you home?" In his gut he knew there was more to it. "Your mom is at the police station right now."

Eli's eyes went round. "Why?"

"She was talking about pressing charges against Jo, for taking you."

Hunter saw fear on his son's face, pure, unguarded fear. "She didn't... B-but... All Josie did was pick me up. She picked me up and brought me here. That's all."

"She took you without talking to me or your mom. That's a big deal. Some might say it's kidnapping." Hunter watched him.

"Kidnapping?" Eli was staring at him now, more tears appearing. "She brought me home. That's all."

He chose his words carefully, hoping to learn more. "Maybe. But she didn't have permission. Did she say why?"

"She said... She said..."

Hunter took his son's hand. "What did Jo say?"

Eli looked at his father, swallowing hard. "She said you sent her." He cleared his throat. "You wanted her to pick me up 'cause you were working and she was supposed to take me to Granddad's. That's all." His lower lip was wobbling. "You really think Mom will have her arrested?"

"I hope not." He frowned. "No point, since you're safe and sound. But I'm not too sure why she did it in the first place."

"She…" He cleared his throat again. "She was acting a little weird."

"Weird?"

"She smelled funny… Like Uncle Ryder does sometimes."

"You're saying she was drinking?" Hunter frowned. "Were you in danger?"

Eli opened his mouth, then closed it. "I…I didn't feel safe until I got here."

Hunter's stomach tensed. He stood up, rubbing his hand over his face. His son, who knew good and well how he felt about honesty, was telling him Jo had been drunk when she picked him up?

His Jo?

Jo wasn't a drinker. Hadn't been a drinker. Hell, they'd barely been old enough to drink when things fell apart. Was she a drinker? It might explain what had happened…

He glanced at his son, at the heartbreak on his young face. If she had been drinking, she'd put Eli at risk. Anger rolled over him. His son hadn't felt safe. He could barely choke out his words. "Anything else I need to know, Eli? You can tell me anything, you know that."

Eli nodded, staring at him for a long time. A few times, he looked as if he was going to say something, but he'd stop himself. All he added was, "I'm sorry."

"No reason for you to apologize, Eli." Hunter bent down and pressed a kiss to his son's forehead. "I'm sorry you were put in this situation." He ruffled his son's hair. "You look beat. Get some sleep."

"What are you going to do?" Eli asked, clearly still uneasy.

"I'm going to sort this out." He shot his son what he hoped was a reassuring smile and pulled the door closed behind him. He closed his eyes, trying to make sense of the past forty minutes.

"Need anything?" His father's voice was low, soothing.

Hunter straightened, pushing off the bedroom door. "Go in and sit with him awhile?"

His father nodded. "Everything okay?"

He shook his head. "No, Dad. It's not."

His father gripped his shoulder. "Well, now, it's nothing you can't fix."

"Maybe this time there's nothing left to fix, Dad." His heart had been broken before and he'd survived, barely. This time, he wasn't so sure.

Chapter Seventeen

Josie pulled the sheet pan from the oven, eyeing the brandied fruitcake. She was exhausted. It was eleven o'clock and she hadn't heard from Hunter or Eli. Every time the phone rang, she jumped.

"You're as jumpy as a jackrabbit." Her father stood back as she turned the tray and pushed it back into the large oven.

She glared at him before returning to the bakery dining room.

"This is my favorite." Annabeth pointed to the peppermint-flavored coffee Lola was testing on the customers. "Very holiday-y."

"One more?" her son asked, pointing at the mini sweet rolls in the basket on the table.

Annabeth raised an eyebrow at him.

He smiled brightly. "One more, please?"

She put another sweet roll on his plate and cut it up for him. "Thank you for using your manners."

Josie grinned, watching the little boy gobble up the sticky goodness in two huge bites. "Someone has a good appetite."

Annabeth nodded. "Gonna eat me out of house and home before he hits puberty."

Josie's smile faded as Hunter's truck parked in front of the bakery. She smoothed her hands over her wayward ponytail and dusted off the flour from the holiday apron she wore.

The first thing she noticed was Hunter's exhaustion. His shoulders drooped, his steps were hesitant; he seemed broken. They locked eyes then, and the look of complete devastation in his pulled her around the counter to meet him. She didn't know what to say, what she could do, but she would be there for him. There was nothing she wanted more than to be there for him, now and forever.

"Did you talk to Eli?" she asked, unable to imagine how Hunter felt.

He nodded, barely looking at her.

"Is he okay?"

"Not really." His voice was sharp. "He was crying pretty hard when I got home."

She tried to take his hand, but he pulled his away, shoving it deep in his pocket. He was upset, that was all. He had every right to be upset. "Can I do anything?"

He looked at her then, raw and defeated. "Jo—"

"I feel so bad. He's so grown-up, it's easy to forget he's still so young." She shook her head.

"But he is young. And impressionable." He paused, straightening. "I can't put his safety in jeopardy." His eyes bore into hers. "I don't understand why you picked him up." His voice was accusing. "Why, Jo?"

She blinked, stunned. Something was wrong. Something was very wrong. "I was trying to help."

His brow furrowed. "Help? How the hell do you think what you did helped?"

She stepped back, glancing around the bakery. "Hunter—"

"Eleven years is a long time. People change." He swallowed, the hurt on his face cutting through her. "I never thought you'd put a child in harm's way."

"What?" She gasped.

"Amy talked to the police." Hunter lowered his voice.

She held on to the back of one of the diner chairs. She knew he'd be angry with Amy—he had every right to be. If he felt it was necessary to bring the police into it, then things must be worse than she knew. "I'm sorry it led to this."

"What did you expect to happen?" His eyes searched hers. "I don't know if she'll press charges or not. But I can't defend you."

And just like that, the floor was pulled out from under her. It was hard to breathe, let alone ask, "What…what did Eli tell you?"

"Everything. After Amy showed up, screaming about Eli missing."

"Missing? But he… Eli left a note." What was happening?

"He left a note, Jo?" Hunter ran a hand over his face. "So that makes it okay that you took him without Amy knowing?"

"I—"

"How much did you have to drink last night?" he asked, leaning forward.

"What?" she gasped. "What are you insinuating?"

"I'm not insinuating a thing. I'm asking for clarification."

She couldn't decide which was stronger, the pain in her heart or the anger rushing through her veins. She chose anger—it was easier to deal with. "What did Eli tell you?" she repeated slowly.

"God, Jo, you can't remember?" He sighed, clearly disgusted.

"Humor me," she snapped.

"You showed up, told him I'd sent you to take him back to my dad's, since I was working late." He put his hands on his hips.

"And Amy was?"

"In the shower." He took another step closer, so there was barely an inch between them. "The worst part is that he didn't feel safe, Jo. He's my son."

She stared at him, pain trumping anger. "Eli said that?"

Hunter nodded.

She sat down then, too blindsided to stay on her feet. Eli had lied to Hunter. He'd made her out to be the villain. She knew, without a shadow of a doubt, he was protecting his mother. Chances were, Amy had something to do with the story. But it didn't make it hurt any less. Eli had lied and Hunter believed it.

Hunter believed she was a drunk who'd all

but kidnapped his kid. He wasn't asking her for her side of the story or asking for the truth. No, he was telling her he wouldn't defend her if she had charges pressed against her. She wanted to scream at him, to tell him the truth, to defend herself. She looked up at him, blinking back the sting of tears.

She stood, pushing the chair in at the table with careful deliberation before she stepped back. "You're a good father, Hunter. Please tell Eli I'm sorry. I never meant to cause any problems for your family."

"I don't understand..." His expression shifted, a mix of confusion and desperation.

If she told him the truth, it would be her word against Eli's. Eli already thought of her as the bad guy. She'd never thought he hated her this much, but still... This wasn't how she wanted them to end up, but she was foolish to believe anything permanent was an option for them.

"Everything okay?" her dad asked.

"Fine." She smiled. "Just saying goodbye."

"Goodbye?" Hunter asked.

"I fly out tonight," she answered quickly. "Lots to do before the move. I am sorry I won't be able to do the mural. I'll let Dr. Lee know."

"Josie—" her father started.

"Tickets are a steal Christmas Eve." She pressed a kiss to her father's forehead. "Lola's waving you over, Dad."

Hunter waited until her father was out of earshot before asking, "You couldn't wait till after Christmas to leave?"

She shrugged. "Dad's better. That was the only reason I was here. The only thing keeping me here. Besides, I've caused enough damage, don't you think?" She wrinkled her nose, trying not to break. It wouldn't help for him to see just how devastated she really felt. She had to get out of here, she had to get out of this room away from these people, before she lost her control and her dignity.

His eyes raked over her, his expression hard and unreadable. "Good luck to you, Jo." He turned, heading from the bakery without a backward glance.

"You, too, Hunter." She choked out the words before stumbling blindly from the bakery, through the kitchen and into her father's house.

"Josie?" Annabeth was calling out.

Two sets of footsteps followed.

"I need a minute," she answered.

"Like hell you do," Annabeth appeared, followed by Lola. "You need to tell us what's going on."

"Nothing—"

"Joselyn Marie Stephens," her father barked, coming up behind Lola. "I want the truth and I want it now."

She shook her head. "It doesn't matter, Dad."

The bell over the bakery door rang. Her father and Lola exchanged a glance before he headed back into the bakery.

"You can't leave," Annabeth argued.

"Try to stop me." Josie sighed, heading toward her bedroom. "You've got Dad taken care of, right, Lola?"

"Of course, sugar," Lola answered. "But I'm going to side with your father on this one, Josie. Annabeth and I won't tell a living soul what's going on, but we're not leaving until we know the whole story."

Fifteen minutes later, Annabeth and Lola were speechless.

Josie clicked the buy button for her eight-fifteen airline ticket back to Seattle, then pulled her suitcase out.

"You're sure about this?" Annabeth asked, eyeing the suitcase.

Josie nodded.

"You don't think he deserves the truth?" Lola asked.

Josie nodded again. "But it's Eli's truth to tell. I can't be the one to ruin everything. And to Eli, telling the truth would ruin everything." She started shoving things into her bag. "I won't come between Hunter and his son."

"Josie, damn it, this is ridiculous. What I wouldn't give to smack Eli Boone on the butt," Annabeth said with a scowl.

"I don't necessarily agree with you leaving." Lola sighed. "But I respect your decision about Eli."

"What?" Annabeth shook her head. "Why?"

"He already hates me…obviously more than I understood." Josie continued packing.

"He's a child. Children think about one thing—themselves." Lola started picking up the clothing Josie had thrown in the suitcase, folding each item neatly before stacking it back inside. "Somehow Amy has convinced that boy Josie is the reason for all the bad in his world—"

"From his parents' divorce to global warming," Annabeth interjected.

"If she comes in there, barrels blazing, and calls him out, she's only confirming his deepest fear." Lola tucked a pair of Josie's shoes into the side of the suitcase.

"Which is?" Annabeth asked.

"He'll lose his father," Josie answered.

"That's ridiculous," Annabeth countered.

"No, it's not. I understand Eli. I was Eli. I was never enough for my mother. Now I'm just like her, no roots, no commitments. His father is what matters most—he can't lose him, too... Especially not to the enemy." Josie scanned the room, finding one red sock under the edge of her bed.

Annabeth sighed, frowning deeply. "It's not fair, though. Hunter loves you. You love him. Eli—"

"Is a good boy. I want him to be happy," Josie cut her off. "I need him to be happy. Honestly, it'll make all of this drama worth it if he and his father come out stronger on the other side of this."

Annabeth snorted.

Lola clicked her tongue. "One thing, Josie, hear me out. You're nothing like your mother, honey. You try, you really do, hopping from place to place. But your heart is loyal. Why else would you still love Hunter? Why else would you still be inspired and happy in this place? If you ask me, sweetie, you're true-blue. Just like your father."

Lola's words left Josie conflicted. If only that were true. Her father was a stick-till-the-end-through-thick-and-thin type. Everything she wanted to be. But if that was true, why was she shoving everything she owned back into her battered suitcase?

HUNTER FLIPPED THROUGH the Great Dane's chart. Maximus was still pretty sedated, but his vitals were regular. He listened to the dog's abdomen with his stethoscope, noting healthy sounds of active intestinal motility and gas movement.

"Let me know if anything changes," he said to Jarvis, one of the veterinary techs who worked in the operating and recovery rooms.

"You okay, Dr. Boone?" Jarvis asked. "You look a little worse for wear."

Hunter nodded. "I feel it, too."

"Isn't Dr. Archer on tonight? For Christmas Eve and all?" Jarvis asked.

Hunter nodded. "Had a few things I wanted to clear up before I left." The truth was a little different. He wasn't up for seeing anyone. Work was a great way to distract him from the pain in his heart and the engagement ring in his desk drawer. Tonight wasn't going to be the Christmas Eve he'd planned on.

He walked along the deserted halls. Except for emergencies, the clinic was closed for the next two days. He stopped in to check on the animals in residence. Mars had left this morning, on all four paws, with her pups. But the other doctors had patients in-house, so he flipped through their files before moving on.

There was a ray of light from under the medicine closet, which was unusual. The hospital had a huge pharmacy, so the door was kept locked at all times. Only a few clinicians had a key, so he was surprised to see the door was ajar.

Amy was inside, loading her bag with bottles of pain medicine and steroids.

"Amy?"

She froze, spinning around.

"Bag." He held out his hand. "Now."

She opened and closed her mouth, then handed the bag over. "I was…"

He looked at her, waiting. "Go on."

She clamped her mouth shut.

"Nothing?" He peered into the bag, whistling softly. "How much is all this worth?"

"Hunter—"

He looked at her, not bothering to conceal his anger as he pushed the door closed behind him. "Yes?"

She glanced nervously at the closed door. "What are you doing?"

"Watching you restock these shelves," he said. "Best if no one sees you doing it." He held the bag out to her.

"You're not turning me in?" she asked.

He didn't say anything. Instead, he pointed at her bag, then the shelves.

"Sometimes you still surprise me, Hunter Boone." She smiled her charming smile before pulling a bottle out of her bag. She placed it on the shelf, then glanced back at him. "Guess it's hard to send me off to jail on Christmas Eve. Not the best present for Eli."

He wanted her gone.

"I was talking to Winnie about parenting. She thinks you're the best dad around." She kept stacking. "I told her you were definitely the hottest."

He wanted her to stop talking.

"Did you know she has the hots for you?" Amy asked.

He didn't bother responding. Today had become one of the longest days of his life. When he saw his key ring, the one he kept in his office drawer, clipped to her belt loop, he lost it.

"You done?"

She nodded.

"Bag." He held his hand out.

She frowned. "I put it all back."

He reached forward and took the bag from her. He dumped five more bottles of pills and several vials of injectable steroids onto the metal counter. "Enough."

His tone must have reached her, because she froze.

"I've spent the last ten years raising Eli to believe the best in you."

She crossed her arms under her breasts, drawing attention to her chest. "I'm not a bad person."

He looked at her, then the medicine. "I'd like to think there's good in everyone, Amy. The last few years, it's been harder to find good in you. I don't want you around our son anymore."

"I have every right—" she protested.

"You have a right to one weekend a month and alternating holidays." He held his hand up. "But this—" he pointed at the medicine "—would take that away."

She glanced at the medicine, then at him. "You're blackmailing me?"

He sighed. "If that's how you want to look at it. I'd like to think we're negotiating how we plan to move forward."

She put her hands on her hips. "What do you want?"

"I want you to leave. Send him a card on his birthday and the holidays. Call me before you call him."

"For how long?" she snapped.

"Do you understand that I have every right to call the police on you?" He stepped closer, his voice rising. "Don't you care that what you're doing is illegal? What do you think Eli would do if he found out about this?"

"He'll never have to," she yelled. "He'll have the Boone fortune to support him."

"If you need money—"

"I do. I need money." She pointed at the medicine. "Rodeo is what I love, what makes me feel alive. I can't give it up, you know? But it's expensive."

"So is spending years in jail. Might not cost you money, but it will cost you time." He shook his head. "I'll make sure you have money—"

"And I'll go." Her voice was lower. "Just don't make him hate me."

Hunter frowned. "Why would I do that?"

She shrugged. "You and Joselyn Stephens—"

He held up his hand. "I'm not talking about Jo with you." He sighed, taking his key ring off her jeans and pulling the door closed behind them. He locked it, pocketed his keys and pulled out his wallet.

"You're a good guy, Hunter." She took the five hundred dollars and tucked it into her pocket. "I know Eli will turn out just like you."

He didn't leave the hospital until she was gone. Once he rechecked all the doors were secure, he waved goodbye to Jarvis and headed home. He took the long way around town, needing the time to get his head in the game. It was Christmas Eve and his son needed cheering up.

The Lodge was aglow with white illuminated lights and a massive wreath mounted on the front of the house. Hunter climbed up the steps and went inside.

"About time you got home." Renata hugged him. "Eli's sick."

"Sick?" Hunter asked.

"I'm not sure what's wrong with him, but he doesn't want to get out of bed."

Hunter looked at his dad.

"Don't look at me," his father answered. "He fell asleep after you left, but he was fitful."

"You left this." Renata handed him his phone. "See if you can get him up for dinner. It's beef tenderloin, his favorite."

"I'll see what I can do." He did his best to relax and smile before heading into the guest room where Eli was propped up, playing his handheld game.

Eli sat up. "Hey."

Hunter sat on the edge of the bed. "What are you playing?"

"Nothing." Eli put the game down. "You okay?"

Hunter nodded.

"You don't look okay." Eli's hands fiddled with the blanket.

"I'll be okay," Hunter promised. "Long day."

"Yep," Eli agreed.

"You feeling bad?" he asked, touching his son's forehead. "No fever."

Eli shook his head. "You look sad."

Hunter looked at him. No point in pretending. "I am."

"About what happened?" Eli asked.

Hunter nodded. "I thought I knew Jo. It's hard when you think you know a person and then find out you were wrong."

"I know." Eli nodded, frowning at his game. "You're disappointed in her."

"And myself. Thought I was a better judge of character." He sighed. "Jo was real important to me, Eli. I really loved her. Next to you, she's what matters most. Losing her again, it hurts."

"You didn't love Mom?" he asked.

"You can love people differently, son. And Jo and I, we're like puzzle pieces. I thought we still fit, but I was wrong." He looked at his son.

Eli's eyes were filled with tears. "You still love her?"

"Probably always will. But it'll get easier in time." He smiled, patting his son's legs through the blanket. "What she did, well, it's unforgivable."

"Dad," Eli's voice was low. "I'm sorry."

Hunter hugged Eli. "Let's stop all this moping around and get up for dinner. It's Christmas—time to celebrate."

Eli climbed out of bed, then grabbed Hunter's hand. "She didn't do it. I'm so sorry. I know what I did was wrong. And bad. I want to fix it."

Hunter looked at his son. "What?"

"I was scared. Mom left me in that hotel by the bar. I called Uncle Ryder and Uncle Fisher, but they didn't answer. I found Mr. Stephens in the phone book and called Josie." Eli's words ran together, his nerves making things hard to understand.

Hunter sat on the edge of the bed, his heart pounding in his ears. Amy had lied about everything, from where she was staying to Jo. It didn't surprise him that she'd lie, but Eli… He looked at his son.

"Josie came right away. The room heater was broken, so she blasted the heat in her car and told me it was all going to be okay. She said I was lucky to have you for a dad and brought me home. I told her not to call you 'cause you were working…"

Hunter shook his head. "You lied to me."

Eli was crying. "Yes, sir. And it was wrong."

"Why did you do it, Eli?"

"I was scared. M-Mom said you'd never let me see her again if you knew I'd been alone in the Roadside Motel. And she said Josie would take you away from me, that I'd be alone. Please forgive me, Dad."

His heart ached, the fear and regret on his son's face both a burden and a relief. "I forgive you. But no more lies, okay?" Hunter waited for Eli's nod before pulling him against him. "You are my son. No matter what, you're stuck with me."

"I know." His arms tightened around Hunter. "I know that. And I feel real bad for causing trouble between you and Josie. She's really… nice. I like her."

Hunter's laugh was breathy. "I do, too."

"I don't want you to lose her." Eli looked at his father.

Hunter closed his eyes. "Oh, Eli. Sometimes you can love a person and it still doesn't work out."

"I know. But not for you and Josie." Eli tugged Hunter into the living room. "You need to go talk to her. I can go, too. I'll tell her I lied. I'll tell her why I lied."

Renata and his father appeared, listening.

"It's Christmas Eve, son. I want to spend time with my family."

Eli nodded. "So go get her."

Hunter touched his son's cheek, awed by the love and support Eli was offering.

Chapter Eighteen

Josie stared at the arrivals and departures board. The green digital letters were updated as flights came and went. She'd been sitting here for hours. She'd been boarding, in line, bag in hand, but she couldn't leave.

Now she sat, staring at the screens, trying to figure out what to do next.

Hunter believed the worst of her.

Eli didn't want her in his life.

Amy was back in Stonewall Crossing.

But her father was getting married.

Her best friend in the whole wide world was right here.

And she was finally writing and painting again.

Could she find a way to be here without Hunter? Could she coexist without feeling that jolt of awareness whenever she saw him? Or smile when she heard his name mentioned? Could she bear it if he moved on, finding love and a family?

She felt nauseous and rested her elbows on her knees. She loved him. She loved him more because he accepted his son at his word, even if it destroyed the only glimmer of happiness she'd ever really had.

If she left… She could move to New Mexico. She'd sign on as one of the Institute's resident artists and teach. She'd write and paint when she had time. So pretty much every evening. It would be a regular job, which she didn't necessarily need but would keep her occupied. The biggest perk was the location. It was the closest alternative to the Texas Hill Country and Stonewall Crossing.

She sighed and sat back, feeling an idiot all over again.

This was home. Why go someplace else like

it when she could stay here with the handful of people she actually cared about?

It was almost ten o'clock. Tomorrow was Christmas morning. She could spend it with her father, watching him open the framed painting she'd done of Sprinkles. She could watch Lola open the scrapbook supplies she'd purchased. And the gift certificate to a naughty online adult store for Annabeth that was a joke—sort of.

From the corner of her eyes, she saw movement. It was pretty quiet, so she glanced over to see the new arrival.

It was Hunter.

Her breathing accelerated.

He was talking to the ticket agent, too far away to hear. The agent shook her head, no doubt apologizing. Hunter kept talking, and the agent kept shaking her head.

He was here. Was it too much to hope he was coming after her?

She watched, her hands clasped tightly in her lap, as he stepped back from the ticket agent.

His hands rubbed back and forth over his face, and he let out a sigh that seemed to deflate him.

He tried again, clearly agitated now. But the ticket agent didn't budge.

Hunter glanced around, the shadows under his eyes visible from where she sat. His gaze traveled over her quickly, almost blindly, before he froze.

She couldn't move.

He strode across the airport terminal, bag in hand, staring at the tile floor, heading directly for her and the row of joined chairs she'd occupied for the past few hours.

He sat beside her, glancing at her.

She glanced at him, fighting against the smile that bubbled up inside her. "Where are you headed?" she asked.

He laughed, soft and nervous. "Seattle."

"It rains a lot." She paused. "What's in Seattle?"

"Someone I need to apologize to." He shifted in his seat, giving her his full attention.

Her cheeks felt hot. "Oh? What did you do?"

"I doubted her," he answered. "And then I let her go without a fight."

Her heart thumped like mad. "But she went. So maybe she's not worth fighting for." Her gaze met his.

"She didn't leave." He rested his elbows on his knees, his face inches from hers.

"She tried."

"What stopped her?" he asked, his gaze lingering.

"For the first time in my—her—life, she realized she had something worth fighting for." Her throat was thick with emotion. She stared at him, lost in his gaze.

"Big realization." His voice was low, husky.

She nodded, incapable of words.

"Eleven years is a long time, Jo," he murmured. "I don't want another day gone without you with me." The fear on his face was so real, so raw... And she understood it. He needed her the way she needed him.

"Okay," she agreed. "I love you, Hunter."

He smiled. "Damn, I love you, too." He took her hand in his, lifting it to his mouth so he could kiss each knuckle, then each fingertip.

"Eli?"

"Wants to talk to you." Hunter stood, pulling her up beside him. "He wanted to come, but I wouldn't let him."

She nodded. "He's okay?"

"He's more than okay. He's ready for you to be part of the family now."

"Now?" She didn't know what now meant, but she'd happily marry him this second.

"Now." His hand cupped her cheek. "You will marry me?" he asked.

"Yes, I'll marry you." She twined her arms around his neck. "I can't wait to marry you."

"Have any plans for New Year's Eve?" he asked, pressing a light kiss to the corner of her mouth. "Nothing like a new year for a fresh start and a wedding."

"And fireworks," she added, parting her lips beneath his.

"I like making fireworks with you, Jo." His mouth sealed hers, mingling their breaths and making her blissfully light-headed.

"I was talking about the fireworks set off to ring in the New Year." She shivered as his lips latched on to her ear.

"I like those, too," he whispered against her skin. "You ready to go home, Jo?"

She pulled back, staring into his eyes. "Take me home."

* * * * *

MILLS & BOON®

Why shop at millsandboon.co.uk?

Each year, thousands of romance readers find their perfect read at millsandboon.co.uk. That's because we're passionate about bringing you the very best romantic fiction. Here are some of the advantages of shopping at www.millsandboon.co.uk:

* **Get new books first**—you'll be able to buy your favourite books one month before they hit the shops

* **Get exclusive discounts**—you'll also be able to buy our specially created monthly collections, with up to 50% off the RRP

* **Find your favourite authors**—latest news, interviews and new releases for all your favourite authors and series on our website, plus ideas for what to try next

* **Join in**—once you've bought your favourite books, don't forget to register with us to rate, review and join in the discussions

Visit **www.millsandboon.co.uk**
for all this and more today!